(Book Cover Tease for Front & Back)

Rising Shadows above the Blemishes is uniquely composed! It encompasses a fresh approach toward handling adversity while learning to excel.

"In order to rise to the top, it is essential to know how to crawl on the bottom."

"Though birds of the air soar high in the sky and are seen by many as they gracefully float across the blue skies with a silken background that quietly endures them, they too must relinquish their positions as many others on the top have had to do in order to be fed."

"Max was viewed by his peers as insignificant, inferior, and a good source from whence to make a joke."

The trials and triumphs that accompany Max are written about to build a solid self-structure for those who doubt themselves.

Read 10 original poems created by the author!
Tears Within the Shadow
Foggy Eyes and Feeble Steps
Create Me Again
I Would
No Lie
Is She
Death Don't Call Me
Check Out Maybe
Blackberry Delight
**Most Notably--Rising Shadows above the Blemishes

Each chapter is introduced with a poem of relevance about its content.

"In the three-room, double-tenant, rented house, lay a beautiful pearl in the middle room. . . . Max walked over to get a closer look while wondering if he could handle it all."

"Upon entering the courthouse and finishing their cool drink, Max noticed three law enforcement officers. . . . One of the three was arrayed in an eye-catching blue uniform . . .Max inquired about the difference. . . . The officer responded that he was an Alabama State Trooper and that the other officers were deputies. . . . Max heard one of the deputies ask the trooper, 'Ya'll don't have none of them working for you do you?' The trooper replied, 'Yeah, I hear we've hired a few, but I hope we don't get anymore.'"

"Max remembers being able to feel the strangeness of her room. What once presented itself as a relaxing abode was now seemingly a noxious environment with a banner of defeat unfurled in its clutches."
"No need to keep on crawling now; be a man and stand up on your feet."

**RISING SHADOWS
ABOVE THE BLEMISHES**

A Book of Encouragement

by Walter Lee Bowers Sr.

Dedication

      This book is dedicated to the memory of my dear sister, Mattie L. Cooper, who through her years of struggle with life encouraged me to seek to obtain whatever goals I desired. Through her diligent efforts, which are superceded by God's grace, I am permitted to share strength with others who may be in need of such. In addition, the love of my unselfish mother, who would always give me her last, continues to sustain me when I am drained. This book is dedicated to her as she wrestles with sickness and the pains of suffering. (I now dedicate this book to her memory.)

      To my precious wife Denise, I dedicate this book to you for your supportive efforts in assisting me in striving for various levels of success. Moreover, I recognize my sons, Walter Jr., Julien, and Brandon, for their abilities to use sound judgment in knowing their father. Your unbroken love for me renders strength.

      For my lovely daughter Anna, born in her grandmother's spirit--blessings.

Introduction

Rising Shadows above the Blemishes is written to build and motivate people who either inherit seemingly insurmountable barriers or encounter them by chance. This book examines and delivers information relative to situations that lead individuals to feelings of helplessness, despair, and the belief of not being able to ever realize their dreams and goals. This book is one that encourages and reveals that no matter how difficult the immediate situation may appear, the solution is well within reach if one would simply realize such.

      There are true revelations within the title, Rising Shadows above the Blemishes. First, in order to overcome unwelcome situations, one must transcend those situations. The situations are considered to be blemishes or marks that are capable of destroying any natural beauty that lies beneath. Rising above such blemishes is essential in overcoming life's adversities. The imagery of a shadow represents the individual who is confronted by such unwelcome situations. When one considers a shadow and places self in the position of being equivalent to such, the idea of rising above the blemishes appears more feasible than imagined.

      This book aims to encourage those who are somehow shackled by life's chances and attempts to reveal to the reader that rising above the pitfalls of life is not merely something that happens by chance, but it is a part of reality that is quite attainable.

Foggy Eyes and Feeble Steps

The wail of the babe blasts loud and long
There's a good set of lungs, child must be strong.
The pretty round eyes are full of tears
Hold the child close, so he learns no fears.
Life is hard, many already know,
But don't tell the child, just let him grow.
His steps are few, and his legs are weak,
Just let him be free cause he's growing you know.
Quite an appetite for a fresh young lad,
He has his own mind, might not be like dad.
The future's over there, he can't see that far,
But look at him reach, he's reaching for a star
Foggy eyes and feeble steps, he keeps pushing on
Better not blink your eyes too much or he'll be grown.
Foggy eyes and feeble steps, let him explore,
This is just the start for him, he'll learn so much more.
Foggy eyes and feeble steps, crawling is OK,
Let him down to crawl awhile, he'll stand a man someday.

Chapter 1
Crawl and Rise

A mother screams and moans with each successive vibration of pain as drops of sweat run from her brow. These manifestations appear to represent inner emotions that only a mother in labor would understand. Soon a child is born who must learn to adjust to a world and society that are new and strange. This new and strange world offers confusion, mistrust and trickery to name just a few of the surprises the child will encounter.

The child learns to adapt to the environment dependant upon the type of treatment experienced from the primary care giver. As the child exits the womb of the mother to enter into this strange world in which we live, little does he know that there are many hurdles awaiting to alter any intended paths of elevation to achievement. When considering his attempts to reach an unfamiliar object for examination, noticing how the attempts are relentless until the infant's will is broken is quite important in understanding the potential for rising above circumstances. An infant will continue to reach for objects, even things out of the infant's reach, because he does not know how to fail.

At what point did you learn to fail? Striving to reach for items that are considered worth inspecting is what an infant does. Babies are slow to accept the idea that they cannot achieve until they are forced to accept such a concept. One might conclude that failure to a baby is the fact that the baby failed to make any attempts in the first place.

An important fact to consider in making efforts to rise above circumstances is the attitude of the baby child. Babies are good examples of how adults perhaps should conduct themselves on the road to discovering new avenues of elevation. Babies crawl incessantly when introduced to unfamiliar settings; the crawling is an important feature that warrants close scrutiny if one is serious about rising above the pitfalls of life's unsuspecting events. A baby's crawling is seldom seen as distasteful but rather is viewed as that which moves the baby toward the desires of the baby's mind and heart. Babies are often praised for their learned abilities to crawl and obtain their desires. Those babes who appear slow in their responses are often looked upon as under-achievers. Crawling is a healthy aspect of the child's physical being. Obviously, the child learns to crawl before walking.

Have you ever considered what a child would appear like if the child had never experienced crawling or being near the lowest level possible on this earth for human existence? More than likely one who never experienced crawling finds life more difficult than it should be as a result of having the cloak of success draped around them too early in life. In order to rise above the blemishes of life, be as the baby--learn to crawl to achieve the desires of your heart. If one has never crawled, rising above those blemishes which will appear from time to time will be most difficult.

A child, after crawling, eventually learns to walk as well as speak the special language that humans acquire. Make a mental note that babies have no particular language or walk of their own. Whatever the baby develops by way of walking and talking is no more than a learned trait, though some may be hereditary, from someone admired most often by the child. The crawling that was done has now developed into more. It has now become a walk that carries the child to greater distances. Notice too that the upright position allows the child easier access to those things which seemed out of reach while the baby was crawling. Remember, while the baby crawled, he also watched what others did. This observation aided him in learning to support his own weight and balance himself, thus leading to the development of walking skills.

The child walks and talks merrily along the way until someone or something knocks him down or hinders his progress. The hindrances may be from other children or adults, but the results are basically the same which include frustration and anger. How does the child rise above these frustrating situations--not having a certain toy, not having that delicious looking piece of candy, being told no, or being spanked? He does so by developing alternatives to that which caused the frustration in the first place.

Now let's draw a parallel from what has already mentioned. Suppose there is an individual who seeks success but is having difficulty attaining such success. Perhaps a good place for the individual to begin is by analyzing the initial approach in his quest to succeed. The idea of crawling immediately comes to mind.

Before we go on, let's clarify the term crawling. Crawling is not to be confused with groveling, for all are encouraged to stand tall yet understand the necessity for crawling to get there. In this book, crawling refers to taking an inferior position in order to attain a more prestigious one in the future. This is necessary should circumstances dictate that one must fall back to a lesser position after reaching the top of the success ladder. When one learns to crawl before reaching the top and if by chance a fall occurs, the idea of being on the bottom will be more tolerable than not having been on the bottom at all. As sure as we are human, circumstances will surface that have a tendency to destroy our motivational drive to contribute to an ever-changing society.

Let's begin by looking at the labor force. Many people remain on the rolls of the unemployed because of a misplaced sense of self-worth. They refuse to accept positions or salaries which they feel are beneath them; they erroneously look upon crawling with disdain. If a minimum or low wage job is available, then accept that job with enthusiasm and creativeness. Buying a

$100,000 home may not be possible today, but tomorrow or the next day may be fraught with opportunity. Mistakes are made when individuals compare their earnings to the earnings of others. First of all, one could be misled as to how the person with the gains received them anyway. When an individual is guilty of comparing money and goods with others in an attempt to measure how successful one is, that individual doing the comparison is headed straight for an abyss which may seem eternal. Upon collapsing into such a situation, rising out of such a pitfall caused by jealousy and a lack of sufficiency is quite difficult from which to recover. The best escape plan for rising above this type of blemish is to avoid getting involved in comparisons in the first place.

One must realize that a person whose net worth exceed six digits is no richer than the person whose net worth is less than a week's salary. Someone might quickly say that any such statement as just mentioned is pure nonsense. As I consider all things, I say that any reasonable person, who weighs all of the assets available to that person, can also make the statement that richness is a part of their immediate status. A person who knows how to manage his finances well, regardless of the amount, is essentially as wealthy as any person with a larger bank account.

Speaking of possessions, they are good to have when obtained through proper means. The proper means consist of elements such as crawling in a low position first, earning your money by honest living, and maybe through inheritance. Unbelievable, the word crawling surfaces again. In order to genuinely appreciate material possessions, one can better do so by having had to work hard in a low paying position which paid only enough money to make ends meet while allowing for a little extra to purchase wants only once in a while. When possessions are obtained through means where every penny counts, then they are more often than not appreciated for their true worth.

Let's look at an example of how possessions are appreciated in terms of how they were gotten. I talked with an individual who had a teenage son. We'll call the son Bobby. Bobby was often given just about anything that his heart desired. Once, Bobby was given a brand new car--his second car to be exact. After driving the car for a week, Bobby became quite careless with the vehicle by spinning the tires and running through the puddles along mud trails and through cow pastures. A friend, who was with Bobby one day, asked him about his reckless actions. Bobby replied, "I'm doing this because I'm tired of this car. I want another one. I know my dad will buy me another one because I get whatever I want, but I have to tear this one up first." One would reasonably conclude that had Bobby been given the responsibility of buying his own car or paying the notes, his sense of responsibility would have been greater. If Bobby had been made to crawl instead of going straight to driving, perhaps he would have thought twice about his recklessness.

Hard work, or at least a good honest day of work, is what is necessary in order to have true richness which enables one to rise above the blemishes of life. If you feel that you are beyond having to rise above the blemishes of life or if you believe that your position is too secure to be affected by circumstances, then continue reading this book. Perhaps a revelation will appear that you too may be in need of strength to rise again. You may be strong now, but what about the times when you may need a lift? The fall experienced may be so great that a quick lift will not suffice but rather a long sustained lift will be necessary. With this in mind, recognizing the ways to rise as a shadow above the blemishes is essential.

Earning money through honest means has been mentioned as an important element in learning to appreciate possessions. Honest means are just as the term implies, which basically indicates that dishonest means such as lying, cheating, trickery, and stealing are unacceptable ways of obtaining gain in order to possess material wealth. The importance of honesty as it relates to receiving cannot be overstated, for there are those who perhaps attempted to rise from the crevices and bottoms through dishonest means and discovered either early on or later in their ascension that the price for being dishonest was a terrible one to pay.

What price, dishonest price, would you pay to gain treasures or fame to experience a temporary boost from the depths of unwelcome situations? Would you consider alternatives to dishonest approaches, or do you believe that the lure of the possibilities would be too appealing to take a chance on losing out? Remember, though birds of the air soar high in the sky and are seen by many as they so gracefully float across the blue skies with a silken background that quietly endures them, they too must eventually relinquish their positions as so many others on the top have had to do in order to be fed. One good fact about the birds is that they have not forgotten how to come back to earth; on the other hand, many high-flying individuals have been flying above earth and others for so long until many of them, sadly, will perish when the true reality of returning to earth sets in.

One must understand that the solid foundation of support is not up but instead is earthen. For the higher one climbs, the fewer footholds remain to lend support. Knowing how high one is seeking to go is important, for it aids in directing toward various goals. However, one must realize that the only true way to rise is to do so from a position of a crawl and then become slowly elevated while rising to the top above obstacles of hindrance.

Anything that is quickly catapulted into space above the earth is likely to or has the potential to be veered from its course, knocked from the air, or affected in some other way by outside or unknown forces. Some of those who inherit wealth, be it money or possessions, are similar to catapulted objects that may be easily knocked out of control. One with a quick vault to the top of the social scale has the tendency to quickly or eventually lose control of self because of rising too rapidly and not having had the opportunity to crawl before flying high. People who fall into this category are often those who view the ones who are crawling as insignificant and believe that society would be better served without the existence of such individuals. Unfortunately, a great fall must occur before the high-flying individuals realize that the low-crawling, insignificant others kept them aflight. In addition to the belief that others are inferior to them, the wealthy, by inheritance, believe that the wealthy should mingle with the wealthy and that the crawlers should creep around together. According to the well-off, this is necessary to prevent the easily acquired dollars from passing on to the crawlers who are not worthy of tasting a piece of richness to relieve some of their pain and discomfort.

To the crawlers, with undaunted faith in yourself and clean living, you can rise as a shadow from the blemishes. The pie that is served for the wealthy, the pie of life's pleasures, is mistakenly thought to be too sweet for individuals who are unable to travel in certain social circles or live in the exclusive zip codes. However, the richness of the pie will eventually cause heartburn and pain for those with the pampered palates. The realization will set in that through all of the flying over others, even rich folks cannot escape indigestion.

Are you willing to crawl in order to rise to a state of being that cannot be taken from you regardless of the adversities of life that may confront you? Being able to rise above circumstances requires discipline that is compacted with dedication and a genuine desire to produce and achieve. Nothing in life is free. Material possessions do not make life, but while individuals live, they would like to partake of some of the pleasures offered. Being persistent is very important and required while crawling from a low status to a higher one. If you are unemployed, the first step is to decide that you want to do something to change your status. Notice that I said the first step is to want to do something to move from the ranks of the unemployed. If an individual is not working and has no desire to change that non-working status, then all of the job opportunities offered will be of no use because of a lack of desire to change the negative status. The unemployed status is classified as negative because individuals are usually out of work because of their own drives. This is not to say that those who fell victim to downsizing and a shrinking economy are out of work because of their own choices, but those who choose to remain unemployed are more often than not out of work because of complacency with being unemployed. I concur with the rich when they conclude the crawlers remain because they choose such positions.

After having the desire to work, the individual must then decide that work is what he is going to do. He must be convicted within and put forth all possible efforts to fulfill the conviction for employment. Setting out to find employment must be carefully done. If one knows that applying for a position of Legal Assistant requires a certain criteria such as a minimum education level, specialized training, or experience, then applying for the position with a lack of qualifications would be futile. However, if the individual desires to be a legal assistant or an attorney, the individual should not conclude that such a position is impossible to obtain. A good approach is to set out moving with a crawl. Start by finding a job that you are qualified for even if it means frying chicken, delivering pizzas, or sweeping the floor. If you don't have an automobile, try to find a job within walking distance of your home. Granted, it may be a low-wage position. If the organization is hiring and you go in with a neat appearance and indicate that you have a desire and a need to work, chances are you will be hired. If there are no possibilities within walking distance, then consider public transportation. If bus fare is a problem, ask a close friend or relative to help you out to get you started. Upon being hired for your low-paying job, immediately start budgeting in order to buy an inexpensive used vehicle that will suffice until your pennies add up. You might save no more than $30 a month, but within time you should eventually save enough to purchase that first economy vehicle. Remember, your pace is one of a crawler, and crawling takes a bit longer to achieve than running or being catapulted. After all, the crawler is doing so because he lacks the ability to sprint. If the crawler could do better, then a different positive approach would be taken. Since that is not possible, the slow approach is taken.

Your employment status has changed, and you are now among the ranks of the working class. However, your need to have the ability to rise above circumstances now starts to take on a greater form, for you are now an employed worker who is considered an insignificant wrung on the social ladder. The struggle to gain acceptance in a materialistic society is now a reality because of accepting a low, crawling position; the quest to reach the top becomes more susceptible to resistance than ever imagined. Individuals who fly high above those who crawl do not think twice about dropping various forms of excrement onto the heads of those attempting to rise above the blemishes. Instead, the individuals who drop waste onto those whom they consider inferior see doing so as a way of influencing and strengthening their own positions, thereby protecting their positions from infiltration from unwanted aliens of a lower status. If you are of such a classification that labels you as poverty-stricken, remaining optimistic is essential. You should expect to be viewed as insignificant.

One who is considered useless by others need not develop feelings of self-pity and shame. On the contrary, one should relate to the others' views of him as a significant indicator that those who choose to label less-fortunate individuals with negative terminology may perhaps somehow feel threatened by the supposedly lesser person's potential. Use the labeling as a building stone to help rise above the blemishes. Rising may be difficult at this point, but a continued daily effort will eventually produce surprising results. Remember, in order to rise one must be totally dedicated to doing so.

I remember learning from one particular individual who often attempted to become a part of his peers. The individual, Max, would spend much of his time wondering about how to become closer with his peers who appeared to have a little more than Max although the peers were not rich by any means. Max's friends would arrive at school wearing the latest trends in clothing. Max, who was raised by his mother, would often report to school wearing what his mother could afford, which meant that Max was not fashionably dressed. Max's jeans were not designer or name brand, at least not of the well-liked, popular variety, but his jeans were the type that were often made fun of because of the initials sewn on the back. The initials read MOS, indicating, according to Max's peers, that Max's mother was on strike (Momma on Strike). Max was so disturbed by the taunting that he asked his mother to cut the labels from his off-brand jeans before wearing them.

In addition, Max's sneakers were very inexpensive when compared with his peers. Where Max's peers paid five dollars for their shoes, Max only paid one dollar for his. As with the jeans, Max was teased by his peers about the brand of shoe he wore. Max's shoes were so inexpensive that they would break apart if he attempted to do too much running in them. His peers referred to them as "slip and slides" because the soles had no grips on the bottom and were very thin. Although he was teased about his inexpensive dress, Max had no choice other than to wear the clothing because that was all his mother could afford.

Max's lunch consisted of processed meat sandwiches or peanut butter and jelly. Max loved peanut butter and jelly, but somehow his peers had a unique way of interfering with his appetite for the delicacy. That special tasting sandwich prepared by the loving hands of his mother was too special to be spoiled by cruel children. Max needed a plan for enjoying his lunch. When lunch-time came around, Max attempted to hide his lunch while eating so that others, who despised processed meat and made fun of the jelly, would not tease him about eating such. Max would hold his sandwich inside his lunch bag, stick his face inside the bag, and bite from his sandwich when the coast seemed clear. Though Max experienced deeply-rooted humiliation and pain as a result of the actions from his peers, he learned to find alternatives to dealing with the hurt. Max would often find solace within himself by conditioning his mind to think positively even while suffering from cruel remarks made by friends. You might say that Max, even at an early age, was learning to rise as a shadow above the blemishes to soften the impact of the soul-searing remarks that burned at his inner self.

Max was in a crawling state of existence, which means that Max was viewed by his peers much like the worker who accepted a low-paying position as insignificant, inferior, and a good source from whence to make a joke. Nevertheless, Max's crawling state would prove to be of great benefit in assisting Max in rising above the blemishes. Max sought an understanding of the cruel behavior exhibited by his peers, yet at the tender age of nine, his understanding was slow in arriving.

From this point one, the focus will be on a nonfictional individual referred to as Max. The trials and triumphs that accompany Max are written to build a solid structure for those who doubt that rising from a low crawl to a state of existence above heartache is possible. As you read further, attempt to become a part of Max and his various encounters and see how it is definitely possible to rise as a shadow above the unwanted torments and misfortunes of life.

Tears Within the Shadow

Though I am young and often not needed
according to someone else's eyes,
The rush of pain that's mine when maltreated
flushes salt from deep inside.
All of this because of my present state
makes me hide my tears within,
So much cutting and slicing I must take
because of the world I'm in.
Who would help me shoulder my days
as I am shunned by friends?
Will you, or you go beyond your ways
to let me be a friend.
Alas! oh No! the truth is now told
behind my back says my friend,
Max should know it or soon be told
that he just doesn't fit in.
Tears from my head flow downward and down
in desperate attempts to lift me,
For peers who wonder, I shall not drown,
My river of tears lift me.

Chapter 2
Max's Tears

The sound of tears of a broken individual such as Max can seemingly be heard smashing against the foundation that supports Max's efforts to rise as a shadow above the blemishes caused by his peers. One of the most painful experiences a person can have is one that is caused by friends.

Max continued in his quest to rise by housing his emotions in a clandestine manner. Max knew that his peers were probably not concerned about his feelings because of the way they often neglected to include him in their activities. By age 17 Max had spent more than eight years with his peers in school and neighborhood encounters. Max was a junior in high school and was still discovering that his peers did not find his company a necessity. Regardless, Max learned to cope with the rejection by finding positive alternatives to the situation. On one particular occasion, Max was looking for a date to take to the junior-senior prom. Max asked a girl, Jenny, from his home room class whom he had known for eight years if she would go to the prom with him. Surprisingly, she accepted the invitation. As fate would have it, Jenny was approached by a group of her peers who informed her that Max would be taking her to the prom in a very old, unattractive vehicle that belonged to Max's brother. After Jenny heard the new flash, she questioned Max about the type of vehicle that he would be driving to the prom. Max attempted to explain to her that the car he would be using belonged to his brother and was well-kept. Jenny did not understand that the 1967 Chrysler was in immaculate condition with a high gloss on its burgundy finish and a clean white leather interior. Still not satisfied that she would be going to the prom in a stylish vehicle, Jenny hinted to Max that someone else had also approached her about going to the prom and that the other person had actually asked her first but was not sure if he would be able to go. Jenny climaxed the conversation by explaining that somehow, miraculously, her first suitor was now available to take her. Max, without surprise at her words that brought tears within his hidden shadow, accepted her feeble explanation. He politely responded to his broken date that since someone else had asked first that she should go to the prom with him.

However, Max knew the real truth that Jenny's lies attempted to veil. Max knew that his broken date came about as a result of her perceived status of him. Max reflected in his mind on how he had asked Mike, his brother, to borrow the car for that special occasion. When Mike gave Max the OK to use the car, Max had a short-lived feeling of euphoria for having arrived to be viewed as someone significant. Max had anticipated giving the car a thorough cleaning and imagined how he would make plans for the pre-prom rendevous with his friends and their dates. Max saw his initial plans ripped from his mind as he accepted the rejection. Even with this, Max learned to rise above the present situation that caused him defeat.

Max was determined to go to the prom anyway. First he had planned to go alone, but he learned that there was another classmate who did not have a date either. Even though Max saw this as an opportunity to undo what had happened with Jenny, he was reluctant to move forward. He had to convince himself that he would not be rejected again. As far as Max was concerned, he was content to escort himself to the prom. After all, Max was accustomed to entertaining himself anyway. For Max, being alone appeared to be the norm. Rejection was nothing new and, therefore, accepting the current situation was nothing different. However, with some coercion from a couple of close friends, Max asked another classmate to be his prom date. Max's invitation was accepted, and the two of them tolerated the evening. Max and his date had much respect for each other, but there was no chemistry to ignite them. Unknown to Max at the time, his determination in finding alternatives, positive alternatives, was molding him for future endeavors that would require much more determination as he struggled to rise above the blemishes in life.

When considering Max's encounter with his broken prom date, it is noteworthy to mention that Max was never really well-liked by many of the girls that he met. First of all, Max was a very thin individual with a crooked front tooth that was caused by his baby tooth not being removed when it should have been. Max had a fair complexion of smooth skin, yet because of his small frame and misaligned front tooth, Max was without any outstanding physical features. Max weighed only 135 pounds as a high school student.

On one occasion in Max's early teenage life, Max and his brother Mike, who was older by three years, had the opportunity to spend the day at the home of a lady who was their mother's friend. A girl, about the age of Max, was related to the woman of the house and visiting for the summer. Max noticed the girl and thought she was cute, but the girl kept close to Max's brother. Finally, after the day had grown old and Max had concluded that the girl liked his brother more than him, Max decided to confirm his beliefs. Both Max and Mike were dressed identically except for the color of the pull-over shirts that they wore. Max's shirt had green stripes on it; whereas, Mike's shirt had red stripes. Max wore black sneakers with green shorts and socks. His brother wore the same.

Max started quizzing the girl about the way he and his brother were dressed. It came as no surprise when the girl stated thatMike had the better looking shirt. Max agreed that this was a reasonable conclusion since there was a difference in color between the two shirts. However, when Max discovered that the girl indicated that all of Mike's clothing looked better than Max's clothes, including the identical shoes, socks, and waking shorts, Max concluded that he was viewed by others as being less of an individual than those with whom he thought he could reasonable identify. Max was deeply troubled within about this revelation. The feelings of rejection pressed on him heavily, yet he continued to condition his mind for survival.

Events such as Jenny choosing to go to the prom with someone else instead of Max and the other girl claiming that Max's clothes did not look as good as Mike's clothing even though the items were identical can cause any individual who is growing during the younger years to develop an attitude of uselessness or inadequacy; however, Max was determined that he was a worthy individual. The feeling of determination wass not without tears and hurt, but while weeping from time to time, Max believed in himself.

Surrendering because of circumstances is something that anyone has the ability to do. Surrendering does not take much effort when one chooses not to attempt to overcome the sections of life that are unfair. When given choices, many people would choose to give up rather than experience the hurtful pains brought about as a result of adverse circumstances. Let me encourage you and say that choosing to press on regardless of how difficult a situation may be is well worth the efforts. The results of your continued march to elevation above the blemishes of life, those things that hinder and oppress you, may not be seen immediately, but if you keep crawling toward your goal, you will eventually rise as a shadow above the blemishes.

The phrase, rise as a shadow, has been used frequently, and perhaps expounding at this point is warranted. When I talk of a shadow, I envision that which exists but yet is not thought much of by those who have shadows. How often do we consider our shadows or the shadows of others? I would venture to say that very little importance is placed on the shadows of individuals. Individuals traverse through this life usually disregarding the shadow, thereby not noticing whether their shadow is with them on a particular day or absent. The importance of the insignificant shadow is just not worth that much consideration. Knowing this, those who are bothered and bruised by life's blemishes (unwanted spots), life's unwanted problems and heartaches, perhaps would do well to consider themselves as shadows that are capable and will indeed rise above all that attempts to hinder them. Such consideration allows individuals to become strengthened through self-determination.

All things have shadows which indicates that shadows are of various forms and origins. This should lead one to conclude that simply because someone classifies another as insignificant or inferior, having the mentality to say, I am but a shadow, and though you may see me as you choose, you will soon forget that I actually exist as people often do regarding shadows, but just as the sun rises above everything, casting shadows to the earth, I too will rise as a shadow of the sun, shining brightly, for I am not commanded to be affixed to the things to which you believe that I should be connected. As a shadow changes its shape and attachment and becomes what it will, likewise I am as a shadow determined and predestined to rise.

The shadow is the individual who believes in self and has a self-determination to overcome all sorts of problems by transcending them all. You must decide as you continue to read this book and maintain an existence in this life that you are capable of rising and you possess the empowered ability to achieve your positive desires regardless of the opinions of others.

The rising ability of shadows is not produced by the direct assistance of others or objects, but it is caused by the presence of indirect actions which aid the shadow in reshaping its form thereby allowing the shadow to proceed to become whatever it will; note that the shadow changes its image by moving from one form of appearance to another. The important fact though is that the shadow takes advantage of its surroundings in order to experiment with various avenues of change. This allows the shadow to determine the type of existence that is beneficial to the shadow and best meets its needs.

When the sun starts to rise during the early morning hours, shadows of different shapes and sizes can be seen. As the time of day rolls on, the sun rises higher producing other shapes and sizes of shadows. A key point to remember here is that none of the shadows have definite names or identifiers that cannot be changed. The shadows may be referred to as whatever the individual chooses to call such. Since this is true, any person who believes or feels that the pressures of life are pushing down too heavily and thus depriving him of golden opportunities experienced by others should start viewing himself as a shadow with the ability, created by life's surroundings, to be or become whatever that he wants to in life.

Shadows are not guilty of complaining about their present state but rather find means of changing as the sun moves across the sky. Should the sun not rise on a particular day, the shadows do not cease to exist but simply recline to another position and location until the sun's light beams again. This should also hold true for broken individuals. When you have attempted to remove yourself from unfavorable circumstances, yet difficulty hinders you, learn that it is important to recline to your refuge until a brighter time when the sun shines in your life again. No matter how small the object may be, there is a shadow; when properly placed, the sun will eventually shine on the small object thus allowing its shadow to show and become whatever it will.

Complaining about unwanted situations is too easy. Often there are those who, for various reasons, find themselves in a never-ending battle against undesirable circumstances which seem to be the reigning champion. The reason for losing though is more often than not because of using the wrong weapons to combat the situation. For example, if an individual who is jobless tires of being shunned by those who are employed, then the jobless person, rather than wishing and just praying for a job, should make actual physical attempts to go out and find work. The tools of wishing and praying without action are the wrong tools for combating unemployment. In order to rise above any of life's circumstances, individuals must be willing to act or react based on the environment that lends itself for use by whomever is willing to exert enough energy to give some appearance of having a desire to move past a present discomfort to a better situation.

Many individuals are handicapped by their own evils and are therefore hindered from rising above their situations. These individuals who blame others for their present status and choose not to put forth efforts, other than verbal, of their own to rise are without doubt shackled in their approach to life and will indeed someday perhaps discover that their ability to rise is stymied. Those who choose to use hatred as a tool for rising above their circumstances should know that hatred is also an improper tool for overcoming adversity. In order to rise freely above negative circumstances, individuals must learn that doing so requires them to refrain from pointing fingers and looking for scapegoats to justify their laziness. The first person to blame for one's state of existence in these modern days is the individual self. If one is not satisfied with his state of existence, then the best thing to do is to change it. Changing a present state means exactly what it says. If you are dissatisfied, identify those areas which detract from your happiness, evaluate the circumstances, and begin working to eliminate the dissatisfaction and replace it with satisfaction.

At the beginning of this chapter, the idea of "tears within the shadow" was introduced. Rising is not a painless endeavor, yet rising may indeed by as painless as seeing a dream. As one struggles in life, sometimes one may find it necessary to shed a few tears. The tears that are shed though should not be tears that are released because of self-pity but rather because of the thoughtlessness of those who would fail to lend a hand in aiding others to rise. Nevertheless, maintain the conviction that rising above the blemishes of life is possible even when there are those who are not willing to lend a hand. I am convinced that there are many individuals who are willing to assist those who are willing to start off at a crawl and work their way upward. Crying within your shadow is good because after discovering your true inner-self, you realize that the tears shed by you are elements capable of helping you to float along in this life while wrestling with circumstances. Cry if you must, but while doing so remember to continue striving for your goals in the midst of all the rivers of tears.

Create Me Again

Silence, Silence, Silence, yet more silence
    as the Creator thinks over me,
He contemplates, without using words, the
    true destiny of my fate.
To what extent should he be made;
    Is he that precious to me?
The Creator moves at his own pace
    determined of the creation's fate.
Now, in time, I do reside
    as I marvel over this creation,
How in the name of the Creator
    did I inherit such a terrible situation?
Hatred and lies, jealousy and lies, working
    hand in hand to crush me,
Oh, if earth would just realize
    that I am simply a creation.
Yet and yet still the world sees not
    and persists in hammering its blows,
Unceasing, relentless, heartless, guiltless without fear
    the world has no mercy to give
The devastation is true and definitely real,
    I fall, I falter, must I forgive?
Hear me as I cry from deeply within,
    create me over Creator, create me again.

Chapter 3
Good Neighbors

In this chapter, we take another look at the plight of Max who has been discussed in the preceding chapters. Remember that Max is a real individual who indeed experienced the situations that you have already read about and the future challenges that you will read. Knowing that Max found ways to face the difficulties in his life should serve as a motivator anyone reading this book. One must realize that no matter how difficult a situation may appear to be or how many problems seem to approach in rapid sequence, if the individual is willing to resurface from the depths of the problems, by being determined to rise above the situation, then that individual has the potential to survive.

Life for some may seem simple, but for others life looks as though it is unfair in every way imaginable. The way you view life has much to say about the manner in which you will live your life in this world. If an individual believes that roses or flowers are ugly and have no meaning,, then trying to gain that person with flowers is basically futile. In order for the individual who hates roses to appreciate them, that person's attitude toward roses must be changed first. The same principle applies to individuals who believe that life is unfair to them. Individuals with this belief must first undergo a change in their attitudes toward life. This does not mean that people must learn to love the elements that produce grief and suffering, but it means that individuals must find positive alternative approaches to rising from that which handcuffs them.

Learning to overcome is an attribute that every individual possesses. The key is learning when and how to apply such. Even individuals who are young in age have the ability to change according to the nature of the situation in which they are involved. Aging, or maturing, should not eliminate one's potential for rising above the blemishes of life because as one ages, lessons learned from previous experiences should help in sustaining one in the midst of turbulent times.

Let's go back to when Max was a young child at the age of 8 years old. Max's neighborhood was the type where everyone in the area knew everyone else. The narrow, unpaved streets produced dust and gravel residue which was regularly blown onto the porches of the houses. The streets were composed of red dirt that became any mother's nightmare when the rains came. Gravel from the street provided the perfect opportunity for the neighborhood children to entertain themselves with rock throwing.   The houses were so close together that the voices from one household could easily be heard by those next door. The dwellings were designed so that each structure held two families. The neighbors shared a front porch which was divided by a narrow railing. The houses were also void of air conditioning with the best comfort coming in the cool of the evening or on a night when the wind was blowing with just the right amount of crispness. Window fans were sometimes used but seldom lasted throughout the entire summer before the motor burned out. The next best thing was using paper fans borrowed from the church.

Max felt fortunate to live in such an area where there appeared to be so much concern for each other among the neighbors. Children were disciplined not only by their own parents but also by other adults who witnessed children misbehaving. There was never any problem with a parent irate because of the correction given by another parent. Max often ran errands for women in the neighborhood. When Max's mother sent him to the store for bread and other needs, he often found himself buying for neighbors at their request. Moreover, items were regularly exchanged for cooking. Sugar, flour, and meal often traveled from house to house. Max remembered how once his mother was getting ready to prepare a Thanksgiving meal but had to wait until the neighbor finished with the broiler before she could really complete the task. Max's neighborhood seemed to him like a big extended family.

As fate would have it, the genuineness of the neighbors' love was put to the test. One summer evening, some time after dark, a man knocked on the door of Max's home where he, his mother, older brother, and sister were. The man who knocked on the door was not a welcomed friend of the family and was denied entry by the family. He was an area drunk who frequented Max's neighborhood on weekends. The initial knock was on the front door of the three-room double-tenant house. After the man realized that his knocks were being ignored, he decided to go to the back door of the house. Again, the man knocked, but this time the knocks were harder and seemed more violent. Naturally, Max became fearful as he heard the knocks and the profane language used by the man. Max could tell by the way he slurred his words that the man was intoxicated. Max could feel his heart beating rapidly against the inside of his chest. With each bang on the door, it seemed as if his heart pounded louder. Max wondered if his heart would break out before the man broke in. A little frail boy with no defined muscle development, but quite developed in will, had to help.

Max, determined to do something about the situation, asked his mother if he could go down the street to get a neighbor, a big man in Max's opinion, to tell the man to leave. Initially, Max's mother refused to let him go, but after the man started banging on the door with a brick, Max's mother conceded to Max's persistence. Max dashed out of the front door racing two houses from his to ask for assistance. While Max was en route, he was thinking about how good he felt for being able to remedy this ominous situation. Max knew that upon arriving at Mr. Sam's house, who was a very close friend of the family, that help would soon be at his house. Max's only fear was whether Mr. Sam would be home.

Max arrived at Mr. Sam's home and pounded frantically on the door. After being invited inside, Max told him about the situation and asked, according to his mother's instructions, whether he would come back with Max to his house, just two houses down, to ask the drunk man to leave. Mr. Sam's wife and their five children were in the room and heard Max's appeal for help. Immediately, after Max had finished speaking, Mr. Sam's wife replied to Max very sternly that her husband was not going anywhere and that he had better go on back home to help his mother.

On that evening, Max learned a mighty strong and painful lesson. Max was of the opinion that his neighborhood was comprised of people who cared about each other. Max viewed his neighborhood as a great placed to live and play. However, after hearing the woman declare to him that her husband was not going anywhere, Max was overshadowed by such a feeling of hurt as he had not experienced before. Max wanted to cry, but even at the age of eight Max knew that his mother needed him and that crying at that moment was just a waste of time.

Max left Mr. Sam's home hurriedly and relayed the sad news to his mother. Max saw the hurt look on his mother's face that appeared to be a look of disbelief. Max saw his mother pressing against the door to keep the drunk from entering their home and seemed to be saying in her mind that she could not believe that her good friend and neighbor refused to come to her aid. While Max watched his mother, he also noticed that the door had started to crack in the middle. The drunk was breaking through the door by using a brick to pound his way in. Max attempted to assist his mother, brother, and sister by pressing against the door too, but their combined efforts proved useless. When they saw that the drunk was actually going to break through the door, they all ran toward the front of the house and out of the front door. This time Max and his family ran to a different neighbor's house. At this neighbor's home, they found refuge until the police finally arrived. The police's arrival seemed like an eternity to Max; in the meantime, the intruder left. Sadly, the drunk who broke the door open was never arrested, for that, as far as

Max recalls. Max doesn't remember sleeping in the house that night trembling in fear as the skeletal remains of the back door were all that was left to serve as a barrier between the hostile outside world and his family.

At this early age in Max's life, he knew that there had to be a better way of living than what he was beginning to experience. Max feared what had happened but believed that somehow he would overcome such. Believing is very important in improving your present state. You must believe that whatever you want to achieve can be done. After believing, you must be determined to do it. Max is a prime example of an individual who was determined within himself, regardless of the circumstances, to rise as a shadow quietly above the realm of heartbreaking situations.

I Would

I would be that which I could,
    but someone said I couldn't.
I would have gone pursuing my dreams,
    but someone said I shouldn't.
I would fulfill my wishes and wants,
    but another told me don't.
I would live a very satisfying life,
    but I heard from another, so I won't.
Wishes and dreams, many dreams and wishes
    often flaunt themselves while flirting.
My desire within craves to give in,
    but I'm told not to by a friend.
I would gladly accept helping hands to boost
    as I try to gain success,
But again as before, I'm held down,
    the advice was not the best.
Oh, I would press on and onward still
    I would be a great man.
I would be famous, I would achieve
    I know for sure I can.
There's only one thing that I didn't see
    while heeding all other's pleas,
I listened to them and heard their words,
    yet I didn't listen to me.

Chapter 4
Afraid of Fear

Overcoming adversities is possible when one learns that the power to rise above difficult circumstances generates from within. For example, some individuals find that catching and petting snakes is a rather enjoyable activity while other individuals are terrified of the mere idea of coming into contact with a snake simply in passing. The one who is able to catch and pet the snake is the one who claims no fear of the snake and believes that the power that is known is greater and most effective in subduing any aggressive behavior by the snake. On the other hand, the terrified individual views self as less powerful than the snake and therefore incapable of retarding any unwanted advances presented by the snake. With this being true, the terrified individual is automatically at a disadvantage and, unless the fear is defeated, cannot safely find an alternative to deal with the reptile.

Being fearful has proven to be a major hindrance for any individual who hopes to accomplish various facets of life's goals. When considering the plight of individuals who attempt to learn the art of swimming with the presence of fear, it is quite clear that such individuals have very difficult, if not impossible, chances of learning to swim as long as the fear is at the focal point of their endeavor. Rather than concentrating on proper techniques for swimming, the fearful individual is more than likely concentrating on the fear. With the fear present, the only thing that the individual will desire to learn is the art of quickly exiting the depths of the water that represents a pit of superiority that cannot be overcome by the fearful unlearned swimmer. The fear prevents the person from entering the water at all in some cases. When this happens, the individual is destined to drown when the need to know how to swim presents itself. The individual has a couple of choices to make. The individual could decide to forget swimming altogether and risk drowning if the need to swim ever does present itself, or the individual could slowly put the fears to rest by accessing formal instruction and concentrating more on the concrete presentations of the instructor rather than fearing the abstract of the unknown.

No one is exempt from being fearful of various situations. The best way to overcome fear is by being determined to find solutions to the causes of the fear. Fear is defined here as a lack of will to confront unknown situations to the point of discovering means of conquering the unknown cause. In other words, when one knows that one is scared of tackling certain issues or potential problems, usually the problem or issue remains because of one's doubt in self of having the capability and hidden ability to resolve the matter. Refusing to recognize that fear exists within oneself is a major obstacle in achieving needed strength in order to rise above negative situations. If one is slow to attempt overcoming various situations, then one must first ask if the lack of desire to improve is because of hidden fears. A diligent and honest self-search must be made in order to discover the hidden fear. The search will prove to be useless if the person searching does not honestly admit that fear, in fact, does exist within himself. After finding or conceding that one is fearful, the next step is to pause for a while to allow acceptance of the idea to become reality. The pause that takes place does not have to be of any particular length. The duration depends on how strong the person is and how quickly he seeks to overcome the problem of fear. Remember, overcoming the problem of fear is simply part of the staircase in rising above the blemishes of life. The problems confronting the individual that serve as a barrier to success still remain and must be dealt with and conquered.

The pause taken by the fearful person may be of a few moments, a few weeks, or longer. The constitution of the individual will help determine how long a pause is necessary in order to gain strength. After going through a stagnant period of pondering over the fact that one is fearful, the next course of action should be to decide that one is tired of possessing an inward fear and say adamantly to self that "as of this existing moment, I no longer care to be shackled and led crippling along paths that I have no desire to traverse, by the guidance of an unwelcome fear that has no right to control or possess." One must say to self that "at this point the control of my concrete destiny belongs in my realm of authority, and therefore this fear that I have come to recognize existed once, but it is no more because the true guide of my destiny is now at the helm of my life." One should say that "sadly I was led along often doubting myself and believing that I was less of an individual than others who seemed to fair better than I, but now I know that for my many thoughts I was in serious error because I realize that my thoughts of second-class status were merely a facade of my fear."After the recognition of fear, the next step is to develop a belief of confidence in self. Chapter Five takes a needed look at the necessity of believing in self.

No Lie

When I think about the birth of a child,
   Amazement takes over and speaks a while.
It says to me to stop and take heed and
   See the miraculous birth of the child.
This is no lie for I speak of a truth
   while peering into the newborn's eyes,
There is something that is strangely pure
   This child's demeanor is sweet and sure.
He has not learned to fear or learned to doubt
   He wiggles and reaches for the sky,
It is absolutely amazing, one can shout
   This child has no fear--he already aims high.
Fears are taught and fears are learned,
   As knowledge is gained each day;
Perhaps one could learn from a child's eyes
   that being fearful is not the way.

Chapter 5
Confidence

"I am just plain dumb and do not have the essentials to be as competitive as others in this world." Life itself is full of competition, which causes highly competitive individuals to advance several steps ahead of those who are less sporting. The idea expressed in the above statement, I am dumb . . ., voices the feelings of many individuals who lack self-confidence. In the previous chapter on fear, it was revealed that fear is a detriment to gaining success and confidence. One must realize, however, that fear is a problem only when it prevents one from functioning in social and occupational settings. Fear may in fact prove beneficial under certain situations. Such situations may include those that have the potential for hazardous outcomes. If such settings are present, then the fact that fear exists may lead one to think twice before undertaking endeavors that are malproductive.

The confidence factor is manifested in those individuals who refuse to succumb to life's roadblocks. It is particularly frustrating when an individual sees his goal within sight, and almost within reach, and suddenly the opportunity is snatched away. Recovery seems impossible after being clobbered by unfair elements. For the person void of confidence, being knocked down or unconscious seems like a good place to stop. This would be especially tempting for those who aren't really committed to success anyway. Life may indeed surprise you, but what a wonderful surprise it is to be flattened and then find yourself getting up to rise above the blemishes. Notice that I did not say it would be good to be picked up. Being picked up is alright, but it could cause you to be too dependent upon someone else. Learning to get up strengthens you and thereby prepares you for any future skirmishes in life.

As a high school student, Max learned to apply his academic talents. Even though he had numerous unpleasant situations while rising from the depths of cruel behavior exhibited by peers in elementary school, Max was committed to using the true strength that lay within. His strength rested in the gift of using his mind. Though not as popular with the mainstream peer groups, Max never lost focus of his goal to finish high school. Max's mother never finished school but would always encourage him to study and required him to attend school daily. In fact, Max was absent from school a total of eight days--from elementary through high school. On the rare occasions when Max had to miss a day of school, he would be quite antsy about being out. He felt as though he were missing something when he wasn't at school. Max's teachers recognized his accomplishments, but some still wanted to disregard his worth because of his socio-economic background. Before you draw early conclusions to assume that I'm about to say that Max was honored by being class valedictorian or salutatorian--stop. Max was neither, but he did excel in English and maintained an overall 3.9 GPA on a 4.0 scale. Even though Max's GPA in English earned him the privilege of receiving the English award, there was opposition by some teachers in the English department. Max had barely gotten by his closest competition with three-tenths of a point. Some teachers wanted to give the award to a more popular student since that person was racking up on awards in other areas. Fortunately for Max, the better side of reason prevailed allowing him to receive what was rightfully his.

Could this have been a breaking point for Max had things gone against him, or would he have had the strength to persevere? Perhaps you have had bad breaks to come your way. Maybe you have missed out on opportunities because of unfair decisions. If you have, you can clearly relate to Max. Life has probably presented many such situations and many may follow. The good thing is knowing that one can rise above the blemishes. Max was a highly competitive individual who cared nothing about losing or coming in last if there is a difference. Max recalled sitting next to a girl in class who appeared to be reading quite rapidly through the pages of the assigned reading. In some of Max's classes, readings were done silently for some portions of the period. Max, in efforts to show the girl that he could read just as fast, started breezing through the pages turning the next one before the perceived competitor did. At the end of the assignment, Max had beaten the girl in turning pages, but he had not comprehended a thing. It didn't matter much to Max because he had demonstrated to himself and the girl that he would not be outdone. Moreover, Max knew that he would read the assignment again at home when he could take his time to digest the material. Max was convincing himself that he was not a last-place finisher.

A similar situation occurred when another girl in his class was completing a writing assignment. When Max noticed how quickly she was writing the material from the board, he knew that he had to compete. He hurriedly scribbled the assignment and slammed his pencil to the desk to notify his competitor that he had finished. As you might have guessed, Max had to contact another classmate later for clarification of the written material because he couldn't read his own writing. The most refreshing thing for Max is that his competition never knew. The only thing they realized was that he had beaten them. Nothing like friendly, honest, high-school competition amongst peers. Max certainly developed a stronger sense of self-confidence. Through continued efforts, Max's speed in reading and writing flourished.

Confidence is not that which comes along suddenly, but it is something that develops through experiencing various situations. There is a confidence that comes about as a result of making the right decisions at the right time, thereby producing good results. Then there is a type of confidence that flourishes as a result of having made some poor decisions with disastrous results, but realizing through repeated efforts that adversity can be overcome.

As a senior in high school, Max considered his future. Many of his classmates discussed going to college and their goals of becoming individuals of various professions. Some of Max's friends were even looking toward profitable lives as professional athletes after completing college. Max never considered such lofty goals as professional sports since he knew he had never been a stand-out athlete. When Max was a young boy, his brother had informed him that he was playing summer baseball with a newly established community team. Max decided that he would also attempt to do the same. This would be a first for Max since he had never played organized baseball before. Max presented with his share of weaknesses to contribute to the team. Talk about being versatile, Max tried his hand at every position on the team. There were games when Max seemed like an all-pro player, yet there were many other times when Max resembled anything but a ball player. Strikeouts were not uncommon nor were missed catches, but Max, through his competitive nature, continued to try. On one occasion, Max was given the chance to start as pitcher. That proved to be a short-lived endeavor. After numerous walks, a hit batter, and several hits, Max was pulled from the game which was still in the first inning. Max concluded that everyone would not go to the moon nor would everyone pitch in the big leagues. Max continued his enjoyable summers of baseball and measured up as an average player.

Not only was Max determined to prove himself in baseball, he tried his hand at basketball, football, and track. During Max's basketball career, he lasted every bit of three weeks. When the initial cut from the team was announced, he was alarmed by the fact that he had been let go. Max knew that he had the ability and skills to compete effectively in such a sport and had demonstrated that he could. Max blamed his older brother who quit the same team a few years earlier. Max concluded that his brother caused his potential basketball career to bounce out of the window. His brother's response was, "That's the way the ball bounces."

Moreover, Max saw a lucrative opportunity to shine in track competition. Max had never run track before, but often he ran to the store regularly for his mother. Max would make quick dashes to the store to get back home in time for his favorite TV shows. Max thought it was very untimely for his mother to wait until time for his shows to come on to send him to the store. Nevertheless, he knew not to argue. Away he would go. In his mind he knew that those mad dashes to the store were sufficient training and conditioning to make the team.

Max's first track meet involved running against students from the rival high school. Max was excited as he stretched on the track with his used track shoes from the school locker room. They were off at the sound of the starter pistol. This was to be the most memorable one mile run of Max's career. Eight times around the small track would be the equivalent of one mile. Around and with quick pace went the runners on the track. Max steadied himself at the back of the pack. Max was feeling great. The last lap approached as Max planned his strategy to shock the moderate crowd of onlookers. The time was right and Max made his move. The clippity-clop of the track shoes against the surface turned to clippity-clippity clop as Max turned on the afterburners. He neared the pack and passed with ease. Max quickly gained on the leader and blew past him with assurance. Max was out front by himself sailing smoothly toward the finish line. Swoosh! It was over. Max had finished first in his very first track meet. What a victory that he could remember for the rest of his life. Unfortunately, although Max had finished first, he had not won. Max was disqualified for passing the lead runner in the lead runner's lane. What a bummer! It seemed as though Max's track apexed early and began a downward spiral. He competed in several other meets, but he never finished first again. Regardless, his confidence in himself was not removed. Max knew that sporting competition was good for the body and mind, but he also knew that life consisted of more than athletic competition.

Max once talked about how a former student, who had graduated two years before Max, returned home for a visit bragging about how he was headed toward a professional baseball career after he completed college. Naturally, this was an opportunity for Mr. Future Pro Ballplayer to ask Max and his friends about their plans for the future. Of course, there was a myriad of responses from federal agent, investment banker, lawyer, and so on. There was even one with similar dreams of playing professional baseball. When Max was asked about his future plans, Max indicated that he was planning to enter the armed services. Max had contemplated going to school but unselfishly thought about how beneficial he could be to his aging mother who had little income. Max's plans were to help her financially even though he had a desire to attend college. Max did not bother to share details about his reasons for entering the service. After the wannabe pro ballplayer heard Max's plans, he looked at Max's friends and then at Max. The next thing he did was to break out in laughter. Max, as on previous occasions, was torn but realized he was becoming a man. Human beings can be so callous in their conclusions about people and their reasons for making certain decisions. Would that person have laughed at Max had he known that Max's decision to enter the service had little to do with concern for himself and everything to do with concern for his mother? Max looked at the immediate situation and knew that opportunities for college would or could come later. As for sports, there was no future for him.

Still undaunted, Max was determined to follow his heart and do what seemed best. One interesting matter of note is to mention that the aspiring pro ballplayer who laughed at Max never made it to the pros. Ironically, Max learned later that that ambitious lad who felt that military service was a laughing matter had joined the Army.

Confidence is being able to make a decision and believing enough in yourself to not doubt your abilities to be productive. Children are naturally confident in themselves. When they are born, they are not equipped with the doubt that enshrouds more mature humans. When you watch children behaving in their natural environment, it is easy to notice that they love to explore. Parents or care givers may become fearful of what the toddlers are attempting to accomplish and step in to thwart their efforts. Parents often want their children to take the safe approach to existing in their environments. When children are shaped in such ways, they are influenced to carry the learned behavior with them far into life. When they consider taking on new challenges, they first ask themselves if what they are about to embark upon is safe. This does not suggest that one should allow children to behave recklessly, but it lends thought to the need to know how to intervene appropriately.

Max was a bit overprotected by his mother. When first approached she strictly forbade him to play high school football. After much pleading from Max and coercing from his big brother Mike, Max's mother finally agreed that he could play football, but she dared him to get hurt. If

Max were hurt on the field, he could look forward to a reminder of her warnings when he got home. Imagine trying to play football without any physical contact! Max did in fact get hurt in practice, but with the help of his brother hid the injury from their mother. Talk about putting one over on Mom--Max and his brother did just that. It was one Wednesday evening while at practice that the incident occurred. Max was practicing at wide receiver. The offense huddled to receive the play from the quarterback. This practice was especially meaningful to Max and the team because they were preparing to travel over two hundred miles for next to the final game of the season. One thing that a player looked forward to was that once a year long trip. This was why many players joined the team. Sure, winning was important, but somehow the bus trip to face an opponent was just as exciting.

The huddle broke with the pass play that had been called, to go to Max. At the snap of the ball, Max was off on his pass route. As he looked over his right shoulder, he could see the ball coming. Max leaped into the air to make the catch and missed it. You would think that it couldn't get any worse, but it did. Immediately, after missing the pass, Max felt a crunching impact from his blind side. He as driven to the surface with potentially career-ending force. The strong safety had made a devastating tackle on Max. Max groaned with pain as he felt a numbing sensation in his right ankle. He was sure it was broken as he lay on the ground in agony. A couple of teammates helped him to his feet, and he hobbled away to the sideline. His ankle may not have been broken, but his spirit was. Max had two concerns: not being able to make the road trip and what his mother would say about the injury. Max's coach had a policy against taking injured players on long trips. Max was determined to go, so he had to downplay the pain. In addition, he was determined to hide his injury form his mother. Mike quickly discovered the injury, but he was sworn to secrecy. Max ran barefoot daily on his injured ankle to ready himself for the trip. Max managed to recuperate enough to convince the coach that he was okay even though his ankle was still painful. In retrospect, Max was glad that he didn't get to play in the game. His team lost several players to broken arms, dislocated collar bones, and sprains, not to mention a humiliating 54-0 loss of the game.

After graduating high school, Max's plans for the future were put into action. In June of 1975, Max was bus-bound to Parris Island, South Carolina, for thirteen weeks of brutal training to become a U. S. Marine. If there had ever been a time to rise above the blemishes, the time for Max was then. He was suddenly thrust into an environment that was as foreign to him as landing on the red planet Mars. Life for Max was about to take a turn that would not allow him to have much doubt about what he could accomplish. Parris Island was an insect infested island surrounded by swamps filled with flesh-eating alligators and crabs. On land, there were frightened recruits and drill instructors from hell. To make matters worse, it was one hot summer with the sun beating down heat rays in excess of 100 degrees. Max's only escape from the one-way island was to graduate from training.

During Max's training at Parris Island, just when things were looking good for him, there was a disturbing setback. Max had the opportunity to become the Dress Blues Body for his platoon. This person represented his platoon in a fine blue uniform on graduation day. It was basically a done deal except for one hurdle. Max had been qualifying all week long on the rifle range. On pre-qualification day, Max scored as a sharpshooter and was only a few points away from scoring expert. This was quite satisfying to Max. On qualification day, something strange happened. Apparently, someone had moved the targets and given Max blanks for his rifle. He couldn't hit dirt with a shovel. Needless to say, there went Max's opportunity to represent the platoon on graduation. Max had resolved within himself that the best thing to do would be to quit the Corps.

Fortunately for Max, it wasn't that easy. This appeared to be the worst situation that Max could remember being in. How could Max possibly rise above such a low point in his life?

One thing Max did was not to focus on what had happened. He realized that there was no way to change the past, but he knew that he could benefit from it. Max made plans for going to his new duty station. After arriving there, he immediately requested to go to the rifle range. With the first opportunity to qualify, Max did just that. He qualified then and on every occasion thereafter. Max completed his tour of duty while reaching the rank of sergeant.

Was there a real benefit for Max in completing a tour of duty in the service? Yes. Max revealed that he gained much discipline by being exposed to a mature, well-structured environment. He was able to assist his mother financially and become self-disciplined. This may suggest a need for self-discipline if one is determined to overcome adversity and reach a particular goal. Without proper conditioning, the propulsion for moving forward may be non-existent. A well-conditioned mind and body is essential when considering the pressures associated with the desire and effort to succeed. Poorly prepared individuals often encounter hindrances that could be debilitating if mishandled. In the event that you are sailing toward your goal and suddenly your ship appears to lose momentum, especially when all seems lost, stop a while. Have you ever considered that there is much to be admired and appreciated in your immediate surroundings? Okay, so the course is not turning out the way you envisioned. Perhaps, it is time to refocus. Drop the anchor and lower the sail, drifting may ease the pressures of the ride. Even with the best intentions and the most-well-thought plans, counteractions can in fact cause delays. So, do you cry and complain about what is unfair or what could have been? If you do, then you will discover that the odds becomes stacked against you. While the sobs and screams are being released without future thoughts of choosing proper alternatives, life continues to rush by. This is where self-discipline becomes invaluable. Anyone can reign as champion without ever having been knocked to the canvas; however, it requires a true champion to reign and know how to pick himself up from the deck, if by chance he were to find himself in such an unenviable position. Your argument may be that you have not had the opportunity to become champ in order to experience being slammed to the surface. You might even say that you've had no chance to reign, but rather have been floored numerous times. May I empathize with you? I do. Yet failing to rise, regardless of the position or lack of position prior to such a calamity, is without excuse. Building self-confidence and knowing your own strengths are essential in becoming empowered to withstand the powerful winds and blinding rays of life. Having self-confidence is not dependent upon how well you can see where you are headed, but it hinges on where you were before you arrived to where you are. If you are able to review your past and believe that it has been unfulfilling, then that means you already possess the inner strength to press forward. If not, you are unlikely to exist where you are today. If life has been quite fulfilling with few setbacks, then surely there is no need to become stagnant with complaints. That ingenuity that you implemented along the way should perhaps assist you in going even further.

Revert to the times when you were young without much concern about life, with plenty of hopes and dreams. Those were the times when you were mentally ready to pursue whatever you thought to be in your best interest. Even though some of the thoughts may have been a bit irrational, the confidence to consider numerous projects existed at a remarkably high level. Unfortunately, for some the confidence needed to achieve various goals shrank or never properly developed because of life's curve balls. Just when you think you've figured out how to foster positive results, there is a major strike-out. There are a couple of choices to be made however. You could gather up the bases, balls, bats, and gloves, and call it quits, or you could wait for your turn at bat again and take better swings. The decision that is made reflects the amount of confidence you have gained or lost in life. Max could have easily given up with the few setbacks that he had heretofore, yet he chose to believe that he could in fact rise above unfavorable circumstances that presented challenges for him.

Is She

She is a young child, born with a lovely smile
She is mild-mannered and has a graceful style.
--Is she the king's daughter and that of the queen,
--Is she the one, tell me, tell everything!
She comes not from royalty, but she is a princess
Her mother arrayed her in clothes often a sack dress.
--Is she then rich now, perhaps famous yet?
--Is she on a home page addressed on the net?
Her fame has escaped her, though famous she is,
Max could vouch for her, she's the sis of his.
--Is she miserable then, because of much lack,
--Is she broken with a load of life on her back?
Life indeed is heavy, a great load to carry has she,
To see her toil on anyhow is quite impressive you see.
--How can she make it over, how will she get through?
--Is she able to carry on, what will she do?
She will press on, she will hold on, teaching lessons for free
she will lend a hand, and give a hand to people just like me.
Is she from royalty, is she a queen?
yes, no doubt, I say she is, She is Baby Lee.

Chapter 6
A Broken Vase

Life might be great if there were no disease, sickness, or bigotry. People could then live more carefree lives and spend less time dealing with stress caused by such occurrences. Since that is not the way it is, it becomes important to share in a bit of universality as it relates to various problems. This is important because people often give up on trying to accomplish things for themselves because of discouragement.

In Chapter Five, you saw where Max showed confidence in himself and completed his obligations as a U. S. Marine. The setting now shifts back to an earlier time in Max's life when he was nine years old. In the three-room, double-tenant, rented house where Max and his family lived lay a beautiful pearl in the middle room. Max came in from school one day and saw this unforgettable picture of the precious pearl. The pearl lay quietly in the sunlight from the window; there was a mystical glow all around. He walked over to get a closer look while wondering if he would be able to handle it at all. As Max went closer he heard "Do you want to see my bald head?" Max eased even closer and heard, "You can feel it if you want to." Max was astonished. You see, that beautiful pearl that lay in the middle of the three-room house was

Max's sister Betty lying in her bed. She had just come home from the hospital where she had recently had surgery on her head. Max knew that she had had surgery, but he did not know the nature of her illness. Betty had been diagnosed with cancer when she was thirteen years old. She was then seventeen. Of all things that could be thrown at young Max, he had to watch his sister deal with such a debilitating illness. Little did Max realize that Betty's handling of such a sickness would prove beneficial to him throughout his life.

Betty suffered from thyroid cancer. She would often have seizures that caused her to have serious convulsions. On one Sunday evening during the summer, Max and Betty were home alone. She had gone into the kitchen while Max watched television. Suddenly, Max heard a loud crash in the kitchen. He ran to investigate and found Betty lying on the floor having a seizure. She was convulsing rapidly. He knew that his mother always knew what to do, but he felt helpless. With fear in his heart and tears in his eyes, Max ran to the front door. Miraculously, Max's mother was walking toward the house as she returned from church service. Max quickly began to feel a sense of relief as he related to his mother what was happening and watched her take control of the situation as usual.

It would be good to say that the seizures ended immediately, but they persisted for several years. Max was taught to pray and believed in God and the power of prayer. Yes, Max was a Christian, and he prayed regularly for his sister, who also prayed for herself. Gradually, Max began to notice a change in Betty's condition. He realized that over the years the seizures had stopped. The seizures that at one time had occurred daily were now nonexistent. Max found joy in knowing that his sister had gotten relief from her constant suffering. There was another fact that Max took notice of also. He realized that during the recurrent seizures and hospital stays, Betty never complained or felt sorry for herself.

Let's examine the benefits that resulted from the illness of Max's sister. First, consider that Max was experiencing something as a young man that produced frightening effects. How did this help him? He realized that if his sister were able to continue in pursuit of her goals without feeling that life was being unfair to her, then surely he felt compelled to set goals for himself and not allow issues to block him in his efforts. Next, he concluded that he had no excuses for not choosing to act upon his ideas. His sister once told him that he possessed the ability to be whatever he desired. Those words struck a resounding chord in his mind. Max also realized that it was important to have a strong will in order to accomplish goals. Remembering his sister's advice, Max decided not to limit himself to complacency; he chose to reach for future goals.

After Max left the military, he found employment at a steel mill. Working in such an environment was not living life in leisure. The working conditions were physically draining, but fortunately Max was was in good physical shape from his tour in the armed services. Every day presented a challenge as to how Max would surface at the end of a drenching ten-hour shift. During Max's time on he job, he often spent hours grinding excessive weld-overflow from the edges of tons of steel. This was accomplished with a hand-held grinder. Max considered that his sore hands, at the close of each work day, were just part of the price for seeking to reach his goals of rising above the status quo and becoming a self-actualized person. Max was the type of individual who was not afraid to undertake challenges even though he was not always able to see the final outcome completely. At one point Max shared the details of his unenviable position at the steel mill with a former high school classmate. The classmate made light of the fact that Max had to make a living by grinding steel. After all these years, Max still appeared to be on the bottom rung as far his friends were concerned, and Max still felt the sting of this piercing revelation. Although Max resolved within himself that at least his work was honest, he still felt the crushing impact of the bruising verbalizations. He concluded that even though he was by no means expecting to be wealthy from his current labors, he was content in knowing that he was in fact earning enough to sustain a living. Max considered himself fortunate to have an automobile and a rented house.

As time progressed, the opportunity for Max to bid on another job at the plant presented itself. Max realized that if he were afforded the new job, he would make $1.81 more than the current pay of $4.35. Max felt that this was a golden opportunity that might not soon repeat itself. Max bid on the new job, sandblaster, and waited for two weeks to learn of the outcome. Finally, the waiting was over. Max's supervisor approached him with he news that the sandblasting job was his. Max felt a sense of overwhelming relief. He was congratulated by his supervisor and even complimented for his dedicated work done with the grinder. Max thought to himself of having no more aching, sore hands at the close of the day. Max could now enjoy his dream job with a heightened sense of a taste of the American pie. However, the newly acquired position came fraught with its own set of miseries. Max soon discovered that at the close of each day he was leaving work in a totally different way. Indeed, his hands were no longer sore, but he was quite filthy from the dirt and grime associated with sandblasting. Moreover, he discovered that he had to purchase work clothing more often because the sand ate holes in his clothes. In addition, the conditions of performing such work were quite unfavorable. During the hot weather months, Max suffered from the heat which was intensified by the hood he wore over his head for protection. When the work was done under cold, freezing conditions, Max had to use all of his wits just to keep warm while completing his task. Max, however, never regretted bidding on the job. He remained thankful for the $1.81 increase in pay and performed his job with as much dedication and enthusiasm as he could. In fact, Max frequently sang to himself as he worked. Max was singing, not because of his present plight, but because he had chosen to elevate his thinking toward future accomplishments. Max had no intentions of sandblasting for the remainder of his work years. While sandblasting and singing away one day, Max was oblivious that he had an audience observing him as he worked and sang. Max's supervisor was standing behind him and had heard him singing. Now before you jump ahead and come to the wrong conclusion, let me tell you that this did not lead to a singing contract for Max. Instead, because of Max's work ethic, his supervisor had come out to ask Max about Mike who had also applied for a job with the plant. When Max turned around and was startled by his supervisor taking in the free performance, his first thoughts were whether or not he had remained on key. Max knew that his supervisor had no complaints about his work. Max soon saw the big, wide grin on his boss's face. It was then that Max's supervisor revealed to him that he wanted to hire Mike. After learning of the news and upon departure of his supervisor, Max's singing became even more intent and filled with greater jubilation. I'm sorry to report that it still did not lead to a singing career. Max was jubilant because his hard work and dedication to the plant had helped elevate his unemployed brother to the status of a tax-paying citizen.

It is helpful to consider what has taken place as far as Max's work habits are concerned. Max needed a job after he left the military with an Honorable Discharge. His accepting the job as a grinder reveals what was discussed in Chapter One. In order to rise it becomes important to crawl. This means that sometimes it is necessary to accept various forms of employment to assist one in reaching a particular goal. Max was not an entrepreneur, but what he had accomplished at that point gave him a boost in his self-esteem. Max's acceptance of the job as a grinder not only helped him, but it also helped his brother. This does not suggest that Max was complacent, for he continued to look for other ways to rise.

One summer Max went on vacation for two weeks. He had remained a part of the active Marine Reserve and was enjoying his time away from the plant. In the meantime, Max had applied to become a state law enforcement officer in Alabama. Max believed that it would be possible to become such even though there appeared to be obstacles in his way. When Max was 15 years old, he and a friend had been riding their bikes through the downtown area and stopped at the county courthouse for a refreshing drink of water. Upon finishing their cool drink, Max noticed three law enforcement officers standing in the hallway. They were in uniform, but not all three were dressed the same. One of the three was distinctly arrayed in an eye-catching navy blue and light-blue uniform. The other two officers were dressed in brown. Max inquired about the difference from his friend who didn't know either. The officer in the blue uniform overheard Max's question and responded that he was an Alabama State Trooper and that the other two officers were deputies. Max turned to his friend and stated that his intentions were to become a state trooper. Again, the trooper overheard Max and responded, "You don't want to be one of us, you want to be one of them," referring to the two deputies. As Max and his friend were walking away, Max heard one of the deputies ask, "Ya'll don't have any of them do you?" This question referred to Max's race. The trooper replied, "Yeah, I hear we've hired a few, but I hope we don't get anymore." Fortunately, the words had no impact upon Max's desire to reach his goal. Max heard the words, but he was not shaken in his belief that good things would come his way at the appointed time.

Max could have surrendered to what appeared to be prevailing prejudice, but he chose to perceive the then-present environment as merely an obstacle, void of the fortitude to prevent him from realizing his goal of being a law enforcement officer with the state. This is a good place to view some of the pitfalls of life that center around differences in people. Without doubt, there are prejudices prevalent among the members of society. Prejudice is not something that evolved on the world scene in the dawn of the sixties, nor is it a phenomenon that will dissipate with the emerging of the new millennium. Bigotry has run rampant since prior to the birth of Christ. Rising above such is not new nor is it unheard of. The problem of prejudices demonstrated by others becomes debilitating when it is allowed to be misperceived as far as its power to limit one's flight to the top. This does not suggest closing the eyes completely to unfair and illegal attempts at creating barriers for others, but it does suggest giving more focus to the planned goal while constructing bridges to go over the hurdles. It is unwise to push the false belief that one is able to change the hearts of prejudiced individuals with the passage of a few laws and creation of various programs. The power of change does not lie in the implementation of rules alone. Along with rules of fair treatment for all being enforced comes the necessity of understanding the differences that exist in people. When we consider the ways of groups of people, then we can conclude that we often react or act based on what we perceive to be true concerning a particular group. When there is a lack of understanding, when the truth of a situation is unknown, when we fail to learn about our own differences as well as the difference of others, then how can we unite toward common goals while not losing sight of individual differences? Consider this. If changes are to be made, then who is it that needs to change? Is it my group, your group, or the other one? If we were honest, we would see that there is need for improvement in all groups.

There are dominant groups who control promotions, hirings, loans, housing, and numerous other necessities of life. But even though the control may not rest within the clutches of the less dominant group, it is essential to maintain the belief that rising above the current situation is definitely possible. As long as there is hope, there remains an opportunity; however, when all hope is allowed to seep away, along with it flees the possibility of achievement. In order for one to help himself, he must maintain a sense of hope. When circumstances are allowed to dictate a person's choices in life, then the person has allowed the situation to become too much of an overpowering force with too much control. Unless one regains control of his own direction of travel in life, he will no doubt be driven and carried to depths that become impossible to rise above.

Max maintained self-confidence. He had concluded that if he wanted it he could have it. Years passed from the time Max heard the statement of the trooper in the county courthouse. From age 15 through a tour with the Marines and while toiling on his steel plant job, Max maintained a deep seated belief in himself. Max's heart and determination focused on rising from the steel plant and becoming a state law enforcement officer. Even though the odds appeared to be against him, he was too determined to know the difference.

Max had made plans to enjoy his time off even though he had to attend military drill. He was having a grand time simply be having a break from work. Without thoughts of the future or magnificent dreams, Max retrieved the afternoon mail one day. He noticed a bill here and junk mail elsewhere. Much to his surprise, there was a letter from the State Personnel Office. The letter was in response to Max's application and test score. He was in! Max read his official notification letter repeatedly. Another opportunity to trek toward the height of his dreams had been realized. Max gave thanks to God and hurried to share the news with family and friends. After he recomposed himself from the excitement, Max thought about the words of the trooper from the courthouse. Little did the trooper know who spoke the words, but he would have a hand in giving Max some on the job training after Max had completed the academy.

The reporting date for Max to enter the academy was just two weeks away. This meant that Max would not have to return to the steel plant. He rushed to the plant to tell his supervisor, in person, that he had been accepted to the academy. When Max's supervisor heard the news, he became teary-eyed. He had grown fond of Max as a person, and he genuinely congratulated Max on his newfound career. The future was upon Max with a bright outlook. He realized that nothing would be given to him and prepared himself for what lay ahead with six months of paramilitary training.

Max completed his training and was assigned to a rural area. Attempts were made by some to have Max dismissed. Little did Max know that he had become part of a pattern of hiring minority troopers and then firing them. This was done in an effort to create the false impression that minorities were incapable of becoming productive and successful officers. Prejudice ran rampant within the department with few people being willing to challenge the practice. Max had just made probation when he was called in for a false complaint registered by a motorist. The motorist complained to Max's supervisor that Max had been rude. Without any articulable facts, Max was guilty as far as his supervisor was concerned. He was never even given an opportunity to defend himself. The supervisor informed Max that he had attempted to have his probationary status reinstated, but he could not do so because the paper work had already been filed with state personnel. Imagine what Max must have been thinking at that point. He was on his dream job and with only six months under his belt, waves of opposition were already breaking against him. Max absorbed the unfounded conclusions of his supervisor and returned to his assigned area. You might think that things would taper off at this point for a little while. Unfortunately, one of Max's fellow troopers reported to Max's supervisor that Max was argumentative. This was done because Max would not take part in making profile stops. Since the complaint by the fellow trooper was too ambiguous to investigate, Max was simply told to stop being argumentative. In other words, be more agreeable and there will be fewer problems. As conditions in the department dictated, the end of trouble for Max was not yet. Another trooper in Max's county reported to the supervisor that Max would not return to his house by the stroke of midnight. There was an unwritten rule that minority officers had to be home by midnight on the day before their shift. That's right. There were double standards present that governed the lives of the troopers. There was one set for blacks and another for whites. The craziest thing that Max had ever heard of was an attempt to enslave him to his position and eliminate any semblance of freedom. Max realized that this was being done in attempts to cause him to relinquish his commission. Max was told by his supervisor to be home by midnight. Since Max had a fairly good concept of what was legal or illegal, Max challenged the discriminately applied rule and refused to comply. On one occasion, his supervisor threatened to write him a letter of reprimand. Max challenged the decision and won. During Max's first five years, numerous ploys were laid with hopes that Max would bite. Max eventually was transferred to a bigger county at his own request. He knew that much had been thrown at him, and he was thankful that he had survived. Max realized that he had grown from needing to crawl to stand and was at a point in his life where he was determined to stand. Not willing to be a person who was disrespected, he became even more determined to stand.

The department that Max worked for was under a court order to hire minority officers until the force was 25 percent in minority representation. Moreover, controversy arose over the fact that there were no minority officers with any significant rank. As a result, Max's employer sought ways to comply with the court decree. Several officers who were in the majority population filed injunctions to prevent the promoting of minorities based on quotas. Perhaps, one could empathize with the he concerns of the majority officers, yet one cannot overlook the plight of the minority members. This created some unrest as fellow officers found themselves in the midst of a friction-filled situation. For Max, who had concluded long before his employment with Public Safety, that hard work and commitment, along with proper self-preparation, were the way to advance, soon discovered that such was all but true. Would barriers of prejudice prevent Max from rising? Hardly.

When the opportunity arrived for Max to test for the rank of corporal with the department, he took advantage of it. After several months of waiting for his results from the written exam, Max received the news. He had scored in the top band and was eligible for the oral process. This would be conducted by a review board. As Max's overall performance was outstanding, he realized that he was now to be promoted. Max's promotion led him to be the first-line supervisor for the busiest trooper post in the state. In that position he was able to gain a clearer view of some of the inner workings within the department. On one occasion Max had the unenviable duty of transporting a minority officer home due to the officer's mishandling of a traffic accident. The officer and Max did not realize it at the time, but the officer was soon to be dismissed. Max's supervisors had conducted an investigation of the officer and concluded that the officer should be fired. The thing that stuck in Max's mind was the fact that there were other majority officers who had handled accident investigations similarly, but they were not terminated. The only difference was their being part of the majority trooper force. On a subsequent occasion, Max had the obligation of conducting his own investigation. He had been instructed by his captain to investigate what appeared to be an unreported patrol car accident by another trooper. The accused officer was also part of the minority population. Max's sergeant was on vacation. When Max's sergeant returned to work a few days later, Max informed him of what was going on. The sergeant, who was of the majority group, began to scold Max for conducting an investigation that he knew nothing about. After the tirade was finished, Max calmly explained that he was following the captain's orders. The captain had instructed Max not to bother the sergeant since he was on vacation and would return in a few days.

Upon completion of the investigation, Max shared his findings with his supervisors. Indeed, the trooper under investigation had been negligent in reporting the patrol car accident. The minority officer was terminated. Max had done his job, but he certainly did not feel the need for applause. Instead, his heart ached as it did anytime another officer was terminated. This was because the termination not only affected the officer but also the officer's family. Max was told by officials from headquarters that he had done a great job with handling the investigation. He was also told that there would be a sergeant's position available soon. Max was asked if he were interested in the slot. Oddly enough, rather than being overly excited about another promotion, Max was subdued because he saw a link between his being perceived as one who seized an opportunity to advance at the cost of a fellow officer's career. Let it be known explicitly that Max did not have a problem carrying out his duties as a supervisor, but Max had a major problem with selective enforcement of the rules. He recalled numerous occasions where double-standards were displayed. Minority officers were terminated for virtually any rule violation while majority officers were either scolded somewhat or totally ignored for similar or worse violations. For example, minority officers were often suspended for overstaying their lunch break by five minutes while majority officers were allowed to sit and eat thirty to forty minutes past their break and often did so with the majority supervisor present. Moreover, transfers were handed down to minority officers who were involved or even thought to be involved in interracial relationships. Minority officers were also quickly reprimanded or suspended for errors on reports or for reports being late, whereas majority officers were seldom questioned for the same violations. Department policies that once accommodated majority officers were quickly changed to hang minority officers. There were even majority officers who committed violent acts while on the job, but they were allowed to remain. One officer was even accused of rape. Evidence of sexual activity was discovered, but nothing was done. Another officer attacked an individual in a public park, yet there were no consequences. There was yet another who became drunk and belligerent toward officers in another town while away on department business. Again, nothing was done that prevented that officer from continuing with his employment. Out of all of the seemingly serious offenses commited by majority officers, the worst thing that resulted from it all was that all of the individuals involved were promoted higher positions within the department.

Max made sergeant and continued with his efforts to make a successful career out of the troopers. Things went fairly well for Max for a few years, but cycles are sure to reoccur. Max had the unpleasant experience of working for a supervisor who despised everything that was done. Max was not even allowed to make the schedule assignments which was Max's responsibility. Max was harassed daily. Finally, Max filed a grievance against his supervisor. In the meantime, another opening had become available. The opening was for the same rank that Max held but in a different division. Max's grievance was resolved to his satisfaction. Perhaps, this is what led to Max receiving the lateral transfer. Nevertheless, Max would learn that his filing a grievance would lead to a different outlook in his career.

Max continued being committed to his profession. Part of Max's new position consisted of being a liaison between he department and others. He often met with civic organizations, schools, businesses, and various government officials. Max made several television and radio appearances. He was efficient in what he did. Max went on to write safety programs for the department that won national recognition at safety workshops. During all of Max's efforts for the department, he never forgot that he himself could use more polishing. Max enrolled in night school at the local college. All of this was done concurrently with Max's role in his new assignment. Max took a full course load each semester. Within two years, Max had completed the requirements for his Associate's degree. Still determined to become a better representative of himself, Max enrolled in the nearby university. By the way, Max had maintained a 3.8 GPA and was a awarded a Junior College Transfer Scholarship. Max pursued a Bachelor's degree in criminal justice and graduated summa cum laude two years later. Max continued to compete with other officers for advancement to the rank of lieutenant. On Max's third attempt at such, he was finally convinced that he had a fair chance of being selected. Max had been a sergeant for eleven years and had a clean record. His evaluation scores were superb with no significant weaknesses. Max also had continued his educational pursuits and now possessed a Master's degree in psychology and counseling.

The position that Max was competing for was finally posted. There were only two individuals who applied. The other individual was a minority with a high school education, one-and-a-half years as sergeant, and fourteen years on he job. Max had been on the force twenty-one years. Normally, decisions about who was selected were out within two weeks. Max noticed that this decision had been held in abeyance for over a month. There was something wrong. He remembered how the other sergeant had bragged to other officers in the post that he would be the next lieutenant. This was done before the posting was ever released. Max learned that promises had been made to the other sergeant by high-ranking officials out of headquarters. Max's competitor had talked regularly with headquarters' officials and had done special favors. Max even heard his competitor joke that he needed a new set of knee pads to stay in good graces of the administration. This eventually revealed volumes of information to Max about ways to rise to the top. Max had learned that self-preparation and dedication meant nothing to the department. The fact that one was educated was of little value. Moreover, Max's experience at the rank of sergeant for eleven years was considered insignificant. Max met with his supervisor and followed the chain of command in seeking answers as to why his competitor was bragging about having been promised the promotion and looking for answers to questions surrounding the selection. Max's immediate supervisor referred Max's grievance to a higher official who was part of the promotion board. Note that the promotion process consisted of a board that was comprised of five majors, who were supposed to give input on candidates for promotion.

When Max inquired about the criteria used to select his competition, his supervisor pretended not to understand. Max then asked more precise questions. He mentioned to his supervisor that he felt as though pre-selection had taken place. He made comparisons with his competitor's qualifications in all areas. He asked his supervisor to consider his education in contrast to his competition. Max was told that there was no difference between his having a Master's degree and the other sergeant having a high school education. Max's supervisor told him that the department didn't require a degree to be hired as a trooper. Max then asked his supervisor to consider his supervisory experience and time in grade as a sergeant. Max was told in response that the only requirement for a person to be considered for the promotion of lieutenant was to be on the promotion list and not to be on probation. He was told that six months time in grade weighed just as much as eleven years time in grade. Still determined to know the justification for the promotion, Max asked his supervisor to explain the criteria used to select the other candidate. The response from the supervisor was, "I didn't make the selection. The other major did." This baffled Max because he knew that the selection was supposed to be done by the entire promotional board and not by one individual. It appeared to Max that his supervisor was unwilling to explain the essence of what had happened. Max was fuming within, but he remained poised and respectfully requested to take his concerns to the final authority within the department.

The next day afforded Max the opportunity to share his concerns with the director, one w whom Max believed would certainly provide understandable answers and an appropriate resolution to the presenting problem. Much to Max's surprise, the explanation given by the director was just as convoluted as the one given by his supervisor. Max was told by the director that he did not know Max or the one who was promoted instead of Max. He told Max that he would definitely investigate the decision of the promotion board. Little did the director know, Max was already aware that the director did in fact know the other individual. The one who was promoted over Max had carried an autographed college football to headquarters and given it to the director prior to the announcement about the promotion being publicized. Max had to wait less than one week to receive a response from the director. In response to Max's concerns, the letter received from the director indicated that he concurred with the promotion board's decision and that he would not reverse what they had done. This came as no new revelation to Max, for Max was aware that he had not gone out of his way to collect an autographed football and hand-deliver it to the director. Moreover, Max knew that he had not rubbed shoulders with other officials from headquarters during driver license checkpoints. What was more enlightening to Max, to help him understand the decision of the director and the promotion board, was that he remembered he did not own a set of knee pads. Was Max angry? How would you feel? Max's dream career had shown the true colors relevant to his dream. Moving ahead in the department revealed nightmarish findings. Promotions within the department were not made on grounds of merit, but they were made based on who knew how to use the ground best. This meant that those who were dirty players were quickly elevated to higher ranks and better positions. In order to be promoted as a minority, one had to have shown a propensity toward abusing other minorities. If one were of the majority faction, then all one had to do for promotion was be a relative of someone else in the department who was a ranking official. In other words, nepotism proved to run rampant throughout the department. It seemed funny to Max that all of the sons of past ranking officials who were hired after him catapulted past him in rank. Max even recalled how there was one individual who couldn't make it through the trooper academy the first two times he tried. That individual made it the third time around and advanced quickly to lieutenant.

For Max, the message was uniquely clear. In order for a minority to make rank within the department, he must be willing to undermine other minorities, show no semblance of decision-making ability, agree totally with the majority, and feel inferior to those who believe they are God's gift to law enforcement. Unfortunately for Max, this was not something he was willing to do. Max decided that it was indeed time to rise from the depths of a false brotherhood and press further toward the horizon of opportunity. Fortunately, Max was in a position to retire from the department, and he decided it was time to move on. He knew that there were some good experiences to be cherished, but he also knew that the department was moving quickly toward the direction of the 1960s with its few number of minorities in the trooper classes and its limited number of minorities allowed to be promoted. Max reflected on some of his accomplishments. He had graduated and received the Outstanding Student in Criminal Justice Award which was subsequent to the scholarship and Certificate of Excellence for outstanding Achievement in Language Arts awards received. Moreover, he thought about having made the National Dean's List for three years along with graduating summa cum laude. He couldn't rid himself of the realization that he had earned a Master's degree in psychology and counseling and even taught three years as a psychology instructor at the local college. Max remembered that he had written award winning safety programs for the department. None of the accomplishments seemed to matter to anyone. Was this the ultimate end for one who dreamed as a young teenager of becoming a trooper? Would his retirement serve as a measure of his final contributions to society? Hardly.

It may be beneficial at this point to evaluate your own responses or reactions to situations similar to the ones Max experienced while on the job. Thousands of individuals from various ethnicities experience unfair treatment on the job. Sadly, too many are pounded into a state of submission that dictates they either comply or be destroyed. As with any attack upon hard-working citizens, there should be an available counter-attack. This means that it is extremely important to make plans for alternative approaches in handling any possible situation. You've probably heard the saying that improper planning leads to a person's poor prognosis. To have a bright outlook, even when looking ahead from the pits of compiled dung, one must possess enough self-confidence and proper preparation to exit when necessary but ready to enter in and accept new opportunities when they present themselves. Max was open-minded enough to know that there were individuals outside of his immediate setting in law enforcement who were more than pleased to allow him to make worthwhile contributions to society. For Max, being a law enforcement officer was not about having the authority to be overbearing, but it was more conducive with offering a helping hand. Max made his share of arrests throughout his career but was fortunate not to have ever fired his weapon at another person. Max was fortunate in knowing that life existed beyond the realms of his department. In evaluating your own responses to situations fraught with opposition, what do you normally do? If you allow yourself to be whipped into submission, then perhaps it's time to go into training. The type of training referred to deals with conditioning the mind. Regardless of the type of career choice that is made, the best plans often face forced modifications. If one is not ready for the unforseen, then it becomes quite likely that the person will be devastated. There are twenty-four hours in a day as we know. Many people complain that there is just not enough time to do the things that they need to do. This may or may not be true. It is a proven fact that when time is managed properly, much can be accomplished. Many waste time complaining about not having enough time. In addition, there are too many individuals burning time being overly concerned about how others use their own time. As a result, very little is gained. Max recalled how acquaintances would criticize him for being active in various activities. They would tell him that they could not see how it was possible for him to work a full-time job and attend school full-time at night. The thing that is important here is that is not necessary for someone else to see what you are planning to do with your life. Too many have had great ideas for being successful but abandoned them when they unwisely shared their ideas with others. In order to move ahead, it is often essential to keep the plans hidden. Max learned that it was not beneficial for too many people to know his plans. Instead of Max complaining about the lack of time available, he chose to take advantage of every minute afforded him. Max knew what he wanted and was determined to get it.

When a goal is set, it is not achieved by simply wishing and hoping. It is not attained by blaming others for being unfair and denying equal accessibility to opportunities. One's goal is reached through hard struggles, preparation, belief in self and God. Max could have become discouraged and accepted his plight as ending when certain doors were barred, but instead he became even more committed to solidifying himself in the satisfaction of self-respect. Many hours were spent studying and attending classes. Max's quiet approach to becoming enlightened through the educational process blossomed with positive petals enriched by seeds sown through the years.

Education has proven to be an important tool in rising above daily setbacks that crop up in life. Max remembered those in his department who appeared to be offended by the fact that he chose to educate himself. Out of all the high ranking officials within the department where Max worked as a trooper, fewer than one-fourth had more than two years of a college education. When one who is educated is in competition with others who are uneducated and the uneducated are the majority, the educated becomes viewed as the one with the inferior mind. Naturally, fear dictates the decisions of unlearned individuals when they perceive others as being threats to their magically acquired positions. When a state law enforcement agency has high-ranking officials who belittle the need for its officers to be educated, it loudly echoes the mind set of those who must make decisions about that state's citizens. The question perhaps is how can an uneducated police force adequately make judgments and relate to educated citizens who live in a world with vastly growing educational requirements. One who denies the need for education and its vital importance is similar to one who has concocted in his own mind that he has acquired all the necessary learning for maintaining an effective life. Learning is a life-long process which says that there should always be a requirement for people to become educated especially when the lives of citizens are at stake. Max was able to rise above the fact that there was opposition to him. Similarly, others must not be deterred because of opposition. The mind must be conditioned to accept certain conditions, but it must also be conditioned to reject others. Rules will often be changed in the middle of life. Players can either quit or continue playing the game. I say play the game. When the rules are suddenly changed, show the competition that you are not a quitter, but rather one who is versatile enough to know how to win.

Death, Don't Call Me

What's that? What's that you say?
No, I don't think so, you bes' go way.
Git back, way back, you hear?
I ain't got time, don't you come near.

I wuz young in dem days in May,
didn't have much, but know'd how to pray.
Early in the morning, sometimes et night
My God let me know, things alright.
I laffed, I played, sometimes I cried,
We wasn't rich, but I had a good life.
I looked at the smile, on Mut-dear's face
I luved the way she sang amazin' grace.
Biskits and serp on saddy mornin'
I ain't skeered, I see the warnin'.

Who dat? Who dat there?
You can't take me, can't take me nowhere.
Git back now, way back you hear,

I ain't going with you, don't you come near.

Let me explain so you'll know,
I's waiting on another ride, We's comin' for sho.
Thought you had me huh, didn't give me a fright,
I'm going home now, I'm riding with Christ tonight.

Chapter 7
Sorrow to Joy

Rising Shadows is written to help others realize the universal nature of their disturbances. As one may be hurting somewhere today, there is someone elsewhere who shares in the pain. The next chapter takes a look at Max as he must rise above a tragic family situation. In Chapter Six, an initial view was given of the middle-room setting of Max's sister suffering with cancer during her childhood and teen years. Miraculously, she grew up to lead a fulfilling life as an adult.

Max's sister eventually married and traveled extensively but eventually moved back to her home town. Max had the opportunity to visit with her regularly as they often rode to worship service together. Max and Betty had the type of relationship that only a true brother and sister could have. It was the type of relationship where they knew where the other one was coming from when wanting to be heard. It was also the type of relationship where big sister would find it necessary to chew Max out for making unwise decisions. She would not try to run his life for him, but she would often attempt to make sure that he did not ruin his life for himself. Moreover, the relationship allowed Max to tell Sis a few things from time to time also. Talk about being close, the two of them could argue on one occasion and give the last dollar for each other on other occasions. Time had certainly produced a solidified relationship from the day of Max touching her shaven head from surgery to the day he stopped by one Sunday afternoon when Sis did not attend church. When Max walked into her apartment, he immediately knew that something was wrong. His sister, who was always jovial, was attempting to be herself, but Max could tell it was all manufactured. Max was able to feel the strangeness of her room. What once presented itself as a relaxing abode was now seemingly a noxious environment with a banner of defeat unfurled in its clutches. The cancer that once intruded into the life of Max's sister, when she was a child, had now returned. It had returned with a vengeance to settle an old score from when Betty had triumphed over it. Max felt his sister's forehead and detected an unusually high temperature. Arrangements were made quickly to get her to the doctor.

As the Lord would have it, Max's mother was able to make contact with the doctor who had treated Sis for cancer in her childhood. They had not been in contact with this doctor for years-- since Betty's earlier victory over the illness. He had moved away several years ago. Recently, Max's mother and sister saw him doing a news conference about cancer on television. The family wondered if the doctor would remember Sis. Sure enough, he remembered her. He took her on as a patient again and worked with her diligently. Betty faired quite well for another two years, but eventually she grew weaker. Even in her weakened state, she continued to give Max encouragement and advice. Day by day the drive to push forward dwindled. Max was working out of town when he received the early morning phone call in June that his sister had surrendered. Max was encouraged in knowing that she had not surrendered to the call of death but to the call of the voice of eternal life.

Would this departure by someone near and dear to Max bring a halt to desires to move forward to reach his goals? Many have failed to complete their plans in life by allowing the deaths of family and friends to devastate them. Death is something that is inevitable. Being prepared is important for healthy functioning in life. There are those who are not able to live because they are too afraid of death. This refers to the fear they have either about their own or someone else's death. Guilt is one factor that prevents individuals from accepting the fact that someone close has died. They may wish for chances to do the things that should have been done while the person lived. Sometimes at some funerals, there are family members who appear hysterical and literally attempt to cling to their deceased loved ones. It would be interesting to see what would happen if no one interfered with their quest. Moreover, they often wail loudly and make statements of how much they will miss them. Guilt is a debilitating emotion that has a power capable of driving people toward the brink of insanity. In order to prevent such overwhelming emotions, it becomes important for family members to care for each other while there remains life in the physical body. Max was satisfied in knowing that he and his sister had shared the best of times throughout her life. Max often reflected on the times they had and learned to embrace the never-ending memories. Max recalled often the words of his sister, "You can be whatever you want to be when you put your mind to it." Death invaded the ranks of Max's family, but death was unable to divide and conquer. Max knew that his sister held fast to her Christian beliefs just like him. Max recalled telling his sister who kissed his jaw regularly, "Kiss me once, maybe twice, but afterwards let me go." Max was saying to his sister that there comes a time when loved ones must learn how to let go and say goodbye until morning.

That particular June saw Max go through his period of grieving. As time passed, Max realized that a new season was upon him. This was a season unlike any other, for it was to be ever void of a precious pearl. Max visited his mother regularly even though he continued working out of town. Max enjoyed the home cooking and opportunities to sit on the porch and reminisce about days gone by. It was quite refreshing just to be home and view the old pictures from his childhood. He loved to watch his mother prepare meals for her grandchildren. She seemed to get much joy preparing for the family. Three years after the death of Max's sister, Max received news that his mother had suffered a heart attack. Max's mother was in the hospital several months but was eventually released. That following November after her release in October, Max's mother prepared a lasting Thanksgiving dinner. When Max arrived home with his wife and children for the holiday, he was surprised at what his mother had done. The family ate and carried on with family fun as usual. By the time January of the following year rolled around, Max's mother was again hospitalized. Her departure from home would never the same. For several more months Max visited the hospital. Again, during the month of June, Max received devastating news. In the early morning hours, Max's mother had departed to a better land. During the time when many would be celebrating the Fourth of July, Max was in mourning. The one who nurtured him and worked various jobs to provide for the family was gone. A fine woman who knew how to love and discipline her family, a short woman who, when she attempted to run across the street, looked as though she was running in place by bouncing up and down, had bid farewell. The Mother's Day card bought for her in May remained unopened. The loss of family members in general is sorrowful, yet the loss of a mother is dreadful. Another opportunity to rise is present as death once again attacks the family ranks. Even so, Max knew that his mother, as his sister, was solidified in her Christian beliefs. Max had enjoyed a healthy relationship with his mother and had resolved within himself to bid farewell until morning. While she lived, Max knew that he had done his best to give love to her.

He was glad that she knew it. Prior to the death of Max's sister and mother, Sis had started the family to doing something that was quite effective in helping Max to rise during sorrow. Sis had convinced the family that they should embrace and share the words "I love you." They had been doing so for a number of years; it proved rewarding. In Max's eyes, he had gotten the opportunity to be loved by a great sister and mother. For 38 years Sis had wrestled with cancer. It never got the best of her, for she remained a warrior throughout.

If one has experienced death in the family, then it becomes rather easy to understand the situation with Max. As Max arose from the shadow of death, so too can others who are confronted with similar situations. Death of family and friends should not serve as an obstacle to prevent one from realizing the goals that have been set. Oftentimes, reflecting on the encouragement that was given by loved ones can be used as building blocks to step toward newer heights. It may prove to be beneficial to give Mom or Dad their tokens of appreciation while they are able to appreciate them. Let brother or sister know that you are proud to be a part of them. Giving gifts is not always necessary because sincere words can be just as effective. Seeing the expressions on the faces after sharing memorable events is lifelong and never fades.

Max continued his quest to rise above blemishes regularly present in life. Max made provisions to take the licensing exam for professional counseling. Max studied daily in preparation for what was to be another important step in his life. He had gone through years of preparation by obtaining the required supervision. Max took the exam, but he had to wait an eternity of six weeks to learn the results. Finally, the long awaited day arrived. Max felt the envelope before opening it to determine how much paper was inside. Max believed that if the envelope were too thin, the results inside would be horrible. With heart pounding and hands wrestling with the paper, Max opened the envelope to read its contents. Passed! That was the word that Max remembered most from the letter. Passing meant that he had not wasted years of his life studying needlessly. The word passed meant that his educational endeavors were indeed of value. For Max, this meant that other educated individuals had determined from a set of norms that Max measured up. No subjectivity involved in the decision, nothing but the facts. Max was elated.

Max reflected on years gone by. He remembered the days of having little to waste. Max thought about the days of his childhood when other children laughed at him and caused tears. He knew that there were times in his youth when he felt inferior because his family could not afford the same requirements for life that others had. When other children were riding to school or being picked up when it rained, Max would get soaked. His clothes were often too small or too big; his hair often needed cutting. He hid his lunch when eating because there was not much in it. He remembered when children conspired to accuse him of stealing another's lunch. Max thought about how he was home with his brother in a rented house when a man showed up seemingly from nowhere and told them that they would have to move. He remembered the meals of cornbread and syrup. Sugar sandwiches were regular delicacies. Days of few friends and sometimes being avoided by the few were revisited. Times when there was no water or heat were brought to mind. Max saw himself going to get the nickel that the woman owed him for going to the store for her. He wanted the nickel to buy for the family. Max thought about his suffering sister and ailing mother, but he quickly remembered they were fine in glory. He was reminded of the state trooper who attempted to devalue education. He remembered both minority and majority coworkers who attempted to block his trek toward success. Max recalled numerous other letdowns with some being even more devastating. Max returned the contents to the envelope and shared the great news with his beautiful wife.

Max knew that he was indeed blessed to have a wife who regularly supported him when others seemed to have deserted him. Max was thankful to God. The closing of the envelope was to be the opening of much success for Max. Max went on to open a private practice counseling center offering counseling and testing services to the community. Max admits that even though he has learned to rise above situations, there is still something that he has not risen to master yet. Max does not like to fly. When asked if he thought he would ever rise above that hurdle, Max stated, "Yes, I'll fly when the Lord gives me some wings."

No matter what the circumstances may have consisted of and no matter how difficult the journey seems, you too can rise from the depths of hollow circumstances. Remember to first appreciate the simpler chances in life which often lead to greater opportunities to excel. Education may not be the only key to success, but it certainly is masterful in helping one to unlock what seems to be a sealed opening to get there. Trust yourself and remember to never quit. The quitting could become contagious and force you to abandon any thoughts of ever trying again. Quitting is easy, yet being creative enough to survive and emerge as a true champion of faith in yourself is what paints a real portrait of success. When gains have been obtained through dedicated service and perseverance, looking back over the temporary setbacks and obstacles becomes quite refreshing. Rise on, and let's meet at the top.

Poems from the Heart of the Shadow

Check Out Maybe

The sleep was sound and the covers soft
When I heard the alarm quickly go off.
Oh no, it just can't be; not talking to me.
I was wrestling with thoughts you see.
I had no job and couldn't buy a car
There were some pennies in an old fruit jar.
Today was the day for a job interview
I'm so scared, I don't know what to do.
It feels pretty good and sleeping's alright
Maybe I'll stay here and sleep another night,
That sounds pretty good and maybe I should
A little more sleep does the body good.
Maybe it's okay to just avoid the day,
After all, opportunity can always come my way.
Maybe I don't need a job, working for another,
Maybe I'm the man just like my brother.
Maybe I will strike it rich, hitting the numbers
What a pit awakening me from my deep slumber.
The sun is shining brightly now, not a cloud in the sky
Maybe I'd better rise up, before life passes me by.

Blackberry Delight

In the calm of the morning
when all were at peace
Mom crept to the kitchen
to make something sweet.
With very little noise, she quietly began
to stir the butter with her own hand.
A little while later
the dish started to cook,
The amazing thing about it
there was never a book.
Up rose the smell of something sweet
The aroma woke us up, had to have a piece.
After cutting the dish
and then scooping it out,
I was eagerly ready for business, tongue watering in my mouth.
It wasn't two or three, but just one bite
I knew I was eating mom's Blackberry Delight.
Such succulence of taste in every last crumb
A might fine talent, where'd she get that from?
Must be from God with his saving grace
I understand now why he called her away.

Rising Shadows above the Blemishes

Tis dark, tis gloomy, tis murky and thick
The troubles of life often seem unfair.
Looking for peace and answers to the problems
I found myself traveling almost everywhere.
Around in circular patterns, I seemed lost and doomed not knowing the way.
Which way is the sky, for I can't look up and face another day.
Sun rising around me on my left and on my right
I don't want to live like this, no more sleepless nights
Too tired to face the day, too lonely to sleep at night
Something must happen quickly to change or I may lose this fight.
Alas, it's nighttime again and things are still the same,
Hark! Listen! didn't you hear, someone called my name.
That one that calls, speaks from deep within

He seems kind and nice and wants to   be my friend.
Why are you lonely, he says to me,
I said, "Because I've been down so long."
He said, "Don't you know the time is nigh; stand up now, stand and be strong."
He said, "You crawled in your early youth when struggling to be free
No need to keep on crawling now, be a man, stand up on your feet."
After hearing the words of this wise man,
I knew that I had to stand.
I slowly rose while unfolding my hands,
I stood up tall, just like a man.
I looked at the sky hovering just above, not very far at all
I started to see my goals were in reach; I just needed to stand tall
Up and up much taller I stood, towering to the sky
Higher and higher I rose above to get my piece of pie.
No more disdain, no more pain, my head's not hanging low
By the grace of God, by the power inside
I've Risen above the blemishes,
risen up like a shadow.

Part II:

Bites from the Heart of a Shadow

A Cover for My Soul

Nights are chilly and downright cold,
I need something, I need a cover for my soul.
Bristling winds howl cruelly in the night,
Its razor-sharp teeth slice through with great might.
Like the hollow sounds of caves on frost-bitten hills
I echo inside with loud chattering chills.
Warmth is not fleeting but has steady fled
I heard some in like situations wish they were dead.
Pitch black shrouding, covering the icy knolls,
I need something, I need a cover for my soul.
Gazing into midnight, windows of ice dim with despair,
Crunching sounds of footsteps slip and travel to nowhere.
Ice! Ice! Ice! mounting further as I go,
I tell you I need a covering, a cover for my soul.
Shivering in the night, I search for a flame of fire
Footsteps are getting pale now, frost covers my desire.
Ice cold sleet pounds and covers the ground,

I search madly for cover, but there is none around.
Weaker and weaker as I break in a cold sweat,
Everything around seems wetter, wetter than wet.
This must be the end as I fall to the ground,
Water still flowing from my head to the ground.
But wait, what is this covering my head?
I have been covered up with covers, sleeping in my bed.
For this I am grateful, it was quite a scare you know,
Yet the good Lord tells me, I have a cover for my soul.

Floating in a Straight-Jacket

The ship was mighty and made from great stock
It has hauled many a passenger, now waiting at the dock.
Boarding such a craft should bring quite a thrill
Many men have sailed her often against their will.
Strange how the sea supports such a ship
Those who ride sat it's one hell of a trip.
They say the seas get rough and cause many a dip
But they say that's nothing compared to riding in the ship.
They're loading up now trying to reach their fill
There are plenty folks waiting, must have been quite a deal.
Anchors away, anchors away, the ship is setting sail
It's moving off and headed afar, sailing toward the shores of hell.
The seas are rough now and the ship is tossed,
There's a man standing there who says call him Boss.
No ease, no comfort is found within aboard this big ship,
No water for bathing and none for drinking, wish I had a sip.
Many free men have sailed the seas and said they really liked it
But for someone who's bound, it's no fun to float in a straight-jacket.

Pencil Magic

With pad on the table, pen in hand, a little time to think,
I felt there was something, something to be said, written with pen and ink.
A bland pad is silent, doesn't mean a thing, while empty on a wooden desk,
But with the magic of a pen, flowing across its face, it speaks upon request.
The deepest thoughts are made manifest as they are carefully labeled and said,
The magic from the pen releases them and by others they're eagerly read.
Letters and songs, stories and poems are written day after day,
All are viewed with perusing eyes seeing what the writer must say.
Joyous words or ones that are sadness filled, may ease from the pen,

Yet because of the magic that's kept inside, you can erase and start again.
Choose the words and write them down, let them roll on out,
You have what it takes to reach someone, just let there be no doubt.
Great writers are among us in every little town, waiting just to be heard,
Remove the cap from the pen, dip the quill in, release the unspoken words.
Pencil magic is magical indeed, there are many who've tried to write,
Hour after hour they sat at the desk and didn't write a word all night.
The key to the magic that the pencil brings, rests with forever knowing
Just start to write, about anything, that's enough to get you going.

Footsteps of a Stallion

Mighty in stature without a shiny, glowing medallion
I race against the odds for I am a stallion.
Known by many to be destined to lead the pack
Hurdles are erected hoping to hold me back.
Competition is plenty as it comes from everywhere
I stride by the rules though others are unfair.
Around winding bends not knowing what's ahead
I pace willfully on daring not to be afraid.
Saddled with hopes that say finish the race
The trots of my footsteps run with great grace.
Steadily moving upward faced with a steep hill
The footfalls dig in as I press with pure will.
Still moving on I learn to adjust my pace
I have run a many miles without making haste.
Easy now, time to glide downward for a while
Must remain focused for a perfect running style.
Darkness is looming and is perched upon the track
I won't let that hinder me, I won't turn back.
I must keep running and jumping ditches as I go
Must keep going for there is a prize you know.
Each day is fresh for I'm not running for a medallion
I am running swift and strong for I am a black stallion.

Reaching From Yesterday

A thought or a glimpse was seen and heard, gathered from yesterday,
I searched and I gathered, pulling from there, pulling for the right words to say.
Yesterday mistakes were made I wished that they hadn't been,
But today being much wiser now, I tend not to repeat again.
Being fleet of foot and quick to know all there is to say,
Now knowledge comes forth as wisdom cries, I didn't know a thing yesterday.

Horizons unknown and pathways have shown changes along the way,
Revelations are clearer as goals are nearer, nearer and clearer than yesterday.
If today were then and then were now, confusion would abound,
But yesterday remains that way, it frees the mind of clouds.
Reaching forth from yesterday, strongholds on life are gained,
Yesterday's pain and pale, dark skies have created strong, working hands.
Reaching up from yesterday, the aim is now centered high,
Yesterday's lonely plains showed that the ground was not the sky.
Reaching down from yesterday, created balance in my life,
Being too headstrong with too much pride breeds misery and strife.
Reaching back from yesterday, I never want to return
Yesterday was a special day, especially now that it's gone.

The Absent Ring

While paving the way on a brand new day,
I was waiting for a call;
This was the day--the chance to excel,
Opportunity would come after all.
 I had prepared myself and felt quite good,
There was a big interview you know;
I had dressed real nice and answered the questions right,
You should have seen it, it was quite a show.
When knowledge is natural and you're born to lead,
There is nothing that you can't do;
Learned how to smile with an appeasing style,
People will take notice of you.

Ah, there it is, the ring of the phone
I was sure that it would come;
Maybe I won't answer, maybe let it ring,
I can pretend that I'm not home.
A second ring, I still will not hurry,
Don't want to be too quick,
If I answer now, that wouldn't be good
I'd better play a little trick.
A third ring and fourth, a fifth
Now I know they wonder,
We had a good man in for the interview
My hesitation makes them ponder.

I've had my fun, I'll ease their minds
By answering on the next ring,
They'll see for themselves that I'm the man,
I can do anything.
What's this?! What's that?! What the . . .

There is not another ring?
"Hello, Hello, I've been waiting for your call,"
I was only playing a trick;
Such eerie silence is filling the room,
I think I'm getting sick.

Seven days now, I'm still waiting by the phone
At least I feel a little better
After all, I know I'm still the man
They are probably sending a letter.

I Still Have Class

Rushing to the country or dashing to the city,
People are so unsettled until it's a doggone pity.
No time to say hello and certainly not good-bye,
People are in a hurry trying to live their lives.
Rude attitudes and pretty dirty looks lurk on people who pass,
Life is fleeting, That's one thing for sure, I'm glad I still have class.

Fits of frustration dominate the world,
There's not much respect, for man, woman, or girl.
Lies are told by many, scheming to get ahead,
It's best not to bank on them, they won't remember what they said.
Trickery and lotteries exist for quick cash,
It's quite nice to know, I still have class.

People are pushing and pulling, steeping on many hands,
Someone cry out, cry out with a shout, let the man over there be a man.
In the hustle and haste with frenzied pace, people often lack tact,
They fail to know that things come and go and life for one is a fact.
In the midst of it all, one has the gall to boast about what he has,
But wouldn't it be great for mankind to say, we all still have class.

Another Utter

Tis hard sometimes to keep a tight lip
One more word just somehow slips.
The flimsy red tongue with teeth out front
Must utter one more word that may be blunt.
Tis funny how when one word one utters
Leads to confusion and offends another.

Soft words are rare and seldom ever flow
Because the last word uttered strikes a great blow.
When words are spoken that pace with haste
The contact of their load brings shame and disgrace.
Loosed from a source void of real care
They are set free to destroy everywhere.
It started with just one followed by another
A blazing hot word that had to be uttered.
It ripped through the hearts of friend and brother
Knowing no bias, it chose to lash at the mother.
Still forging ahead with a pace going strong,
The last word uttered sliced and gorged up homes.
Still undaunted and destined without retreat
The last word uttered looked for others to defeat.
Searching more for other targets to meet
At last there is someone the uttered word can greet.
With much dismay covering a broken heart
The last uttered word returned to its start.

A Lover's Alibi (Masculine)

Loving one and being in love causes one to use his wits,
It is especially true when has been stung and ripped by love to bits.
The heart of one who falls in love must land in the right hands,
A careless stranger could alter its beat and create a broken man.
Many men have loved and learned to regret the precious secrets told
From the chambers of their hearts they freely spoke, but their lover's response was cold.
Trusting and believing, feeling good, from soft caresses on his head,
With great disdain and sheer disbelief, she never heard one word he said.
Seems like enough to cause great men to cry
Yet for some it won't happen, some will lie, some will use the lover's alibi.
--Woman I know you want me because I have it together
--But I can't be tied down, you'd be wanting me forever.
--Yes, I know you called wanting to spend some time,
--However, I am the type of man you see, who has them waiting in line.
--Three calls this hour and five the next, women won't leave me alone,
--It would be great to get some relief, but they even follow me home.
--I have plenty and so much more, for women I'm a gold mine,
--If I heeded the calls and let them all in, surely I'd commit a crime.
Back in the silence of a lonely room, where ticking clocks are heard,
The heartbeat is thumping--growing sadder still, the man speaks not a word.
No telephone ringing, no company to visit, there's a quiet gaze in his eyes.

Maybe tomorrow will speak a bit different, without a lover's alibi.

A Lover's Alibi (Feminine)

So you think you are it with your fancy ride,
Because of guys like you, I don't want to be a bride.
Wherever I go, I hear women speaking your name
They seemed amazed by you, but I know you're just a game.
Nicely trimmed hair atop those pretty good looks
I'm glad I'm not a sucker, for then I'd get hooked.
No time for love, no time for fun, I'm a career woman today,
Why let you in, to toy with my life, when I've already got it made.
Tough luck it is, tough luck indeed, it's past the five o'clock hour
It's time to relax, kick off my shoes, better yet I'll have a shower.
What's this, my heart, speaking to me, while I try to unwind,
I hear the beat drumming out a code that's about to blow my mind.
--Dear sweet girl or woman if you please, why do you live a lie?
--This heart aches and this heart bleeds from a lover's alibi.
--Deep within you want someone with whom to share you love,
--Yet you're too afraid to let them in, you remember being hurt by love.
--It's so unfair to rob yourself of a sincere love you can gain
--It's so sad not to trust again, because of being stripped of love by a man.
Oh pure heart, speaking to me, I hear the words you say
Such true words, such good words, but I am yet afraid.
Tears collect and tears roll down, weary are my eyes,
Maybe tomorrow I will be strong and not need a lover's alibi.

Misplaced Feelings

Meeting that certain someone means so much
When there are special things to share,
The touching of hands while walking together
Represents just how much you care.
But when the hand of one who walks with you
Yearns to be held by another,
Surely this says that the hand that is held
Has misplaced feelings for some other.
As you caress and hold so close
Hoping the embrace is understood,
Distance is felt and the gap is wide
If they could replace you, they would.

While giving love and laughing out loud
Desperately trying to create a bond,
Misplaced feelings send a message that says
Thanks for trying, but you're not the one.
Reaching out to fill the void
Created by a mate
Makes it hard to love and be loved
When feelings are misplaced.

Square Love

Your beauty has lured me and I must take note,
There is a sparkle about you of which many wrote.
The glow from your face illuminates me with shame,
I remember when we met how you quietly spoke my name.
Whenever you speak to me, the sound I love to hear,
Is your soft voice saying words that only I can hear.
Your eyes have assured me that you know how to love,
The halo about you says you were sent to me--my love.
Such gracefulness in your walk says that you know,
Beauty such as yours was just made to flow.
Flowers that bloom grow with hopes to compete,
But as your beauty flourishes, they go down in defeat.
The sun shines brightly except on cloudy days,
Yet the glow, about you, chases the clouds away.
Kissing your lips...sweet, ever so sweet,
Giving your love to me makes a square complete.

Practical Love

Being in love leads you to say
Many beautiful things.
But may I say in just plain words
I love you, you're my queen.
I would love to say I'd give the world,
But that I cannot do.
Even though the world is not mine,
I still say I love you.
Many can spend their very last dime
Trying hard to impress,

I'm sorry but I have a few bills,
I'll save and give my best.
Fine dining is nice, it's good to be
In a place away from home,
But I'd love to prepare a meal for you
At home all alone.
Many move quickly, forge on ahead,
Sweeping lovers off their feet.
But my style is slow, I want you to know,
I rise slowly to the peak.
Allow me to be practical
And maybe you'll say,
We've grown now to love each other,
Because we grew along the way.

Backyard Love

I long to speak from my heart to you
I have a love that is meant just for us two.
A sincere love that has a special part
It's the kind of love seen only in the backyard.
In the backyard there are wonderful things,
Everlasting times that only true love brings.
Whether day or night, morning or noon,
I can always hear a most loverly tune.
The sound of your voice speaking with joy
Reassures my heart that I've made the right choice.
Sitting on the steps while stroking your hair
Let's me feel the warmth that says you care.
In the backyard, there are flowers that grow,
Though they lose their petals, you forever glow.
Holding hands while walking in bare feet
Draws us closer while caressing under a tree.
As the moment speaks about wedded bliss
We are moved together to share a kiss.
Holding and touching as the flames of love grow
It's such a wonderful feeling that only lovers know.
Many have said that beauty is like a dove
But there is nothing more beautiful than backyard love.

Don't Say Good-Bye

When your love for me is gone

As life moves on--Don't Say Good-Bye.
When tender moments are done
And I'm not the one--Don't Say Good-Bye.
If tears fill my eyes
While I'm torn inside--Don't Say Good-Bye.
If the fun times we had
No longer last--Don't Say Good-Bye.
When there is emptiness around
And we make no sounds--Don't Say Good-Bye.
When I can't hold you in my arms
And have lost my charm--Don't Say Good-Bye.
Good-bye is a sad phrase that lingers in the air
If you say good-bye, I'll hear the words, echoing everywhere.
If time says that you must leave and depart from my sight,
Then leave you must, I may understand, just kiss me sweet goodnight.
After our embrace, I'll walk away, holding the tears inside,
I love you my dear, now on your way, just Don't Say Good-Bye.

Anyway Love

Loving you is a wonderful thing.
Because we have each other.
We share what only love can bring
We're friends and yet we're lovers.
We may not have a warm fireplace
To cuddle in front of a fire,
We have many blankets and quilts,
Passion heats our hearts' desire.
We may not have money to burn
Traveling to far away lands,
But we are rich, rich with each other
We travel when we can.
Anyway Love, Anyway we can
We'll keep loving each other,
Anyway Love, Anyway we can
We'll grow in love together.
Loving you is a wonderful thing,
I'm glad you invited me in.
Anyway you allow me to love,
I want to love you over again.

What a World

What a world it must have been, created out of nothing,
What a world it must have been, created out of nothing!
Herbs and trees to man's delight, such pleasure found therein,
Man and woman sharing together as husband, wife, and friends.
What a world it must have been, advancements everywhere,
People sailing from miles abroad wearing inquisitive stares.
Deals are made and papers are signed sealing up the deals,
Land's being bought and taken by force while others work the fields.
What a world it must have been as greed gained great ground,
Settlers building but never satisfied they had to break new ground,
Upward and out great cities emerged, towering up everywhere.
What a world it must have been as pollution filled the air.
What a world it must have been, when people were not the same
Some men were honored while some were torn by treatment inhumane.
What a world it must have been, when nations rose against nation,
What a world it must have been when man ruined God's creation.
In the sky bright lights are flaring, but it's not star, moon, or sun
Flashing lights and twinkling sights are missiles on the run.
Hissing noise and bursting sounds are not the tunes of thunder
Listen closely and you will hear the ruins of man's own blunder.
What a world it must have been, when there were gentle boys and girls,
What a world it must have been, when there once was a world.

A Broken Railroad Track

When young in age, with growing strength, I walked down the track
There was no worry, no fear in my heart, the track would take me back.
Exploring was great, I saw sights unknown, wonders were everywhere
I touched, I walked, I sought and stared, I was glad just to be there.
Broken bottles and rusty, crushed cans lay strewn about the land,
No deer were darting, no rivers flowing, was not a beached filled with sand.
No manicured lawns or skyscrapers tall were seen from this place,
The only thing that seemed rather tall was bushes growing without shape.
While viewing all the wonderful sights along the railroad track,
I was glad that I had a home and the tracks would lead me back.
In the home was peace and love, joy was found therein
Time leaped on, when I was grown, I decided to go home again.
Walking back up that railroad track, I started looking for the end
Much to my hurt, the track had been broken, I never found home again.
No apple pies, no aromas sweet, were ever to be known in there,
They once were known, but now they're gone, they were indeed quite rare.
Walking up a railroad track that led and now is broken,
Helps one to realize--it's good--the words I love you were spoken.